Forgetting How to Breathe

A NOVEL

ANITA DAHER

yellow dog

Yellow Dog
(an imprint of Great Plains Publications)
1173 Wolseley Avenue
Winnipeg, MB R3G 1H1
www.greatplains.mb.ca

Great Plains Publications gratefully acknowledges the financial support
provided for its publishing program by the Government of Canada
through the Canada Book Fund; the Canada Council for the Arts;
the Province of Manitoba through the Book Publishing Tax Credit
and the Book Publisher Marketing Assistance Program; and the
Manitoba Arts Council.

Design & Typography by Relish New Brand Experience
Printed in Canada by Friesens
Cover image of children by photographer David Jordan, Leeds UK

LIBRARY AND ARCHIVES CANADA CATALOGUING IN PUBLICATION

Daher, Anita, 1965-, author
    Forgetting how to breathe / Anita Daher.

Issued in print and electronic formats.
ISBN 978-1-927855-91-1 (softcover).--ISBN 978-1-927855-92-8 (EPUB).--
ISBN 978-1-927855-93-5 (Kindle)

    1. Title.

PS8557.A35F67 2018   jC813'.6   C2017-907259-5
                                              C2017-907260-9

ENVIRONMENTAL BENEFITS STATEMENT

Great Plains Publications saved the following
resources by printing the pages of this book on
chlorine free paper made with 100% post-consumer
waste.

TREES	WATER	ENERGY	SOLID WASTE	GREENHOUSE GASES
3	1,211	2	82	223
FULLY GROWN	GALLONS	MILLION BTUs	POUNDS	POUNDS

Environmental impact estimates were made using the Environmental Paper Network
Paper Calculator 3.2. For more information visit www.papercalculator.org.

FSC
www.fsc.org
MIX
Paper from
responsible sources
FSC® C016245

Flóki-Vilgerðarsson loosed the ravens at sea. The first flew up and turned back the way they'd come. The second spread its wings and soared high, circled the area around the boat, and returned without the news they sought. The third led the way sure and steady toward land.

—LOOSELY TRANSLATED FROM THE MEDIEVAL MANUSCRIPT, *LANDNÁMABÓK*, THE ICELANDIC BOOK OF SETTLEMENTS

Chapter One

Tia struggled to keep exasperation from her voice. "Come on, Tag. I told you we have to hurry."

"But I don't *want* to hitch a ride," Tag whined. "Can't we take a bus?"

Her brother's complaining was beginning to grate on her last nerve. She knew it was because he was scared—and only eight years old. With all they'd been through, she sometimes forgot that he was still a little kid. But what choice did they have? Winnipeg was a one-hour drive from their new home in Manitoba's Interlake. Too far to walk.

"There is no bus," Tia told him. "Anyway, it's Friday night. Lots of people will be driving to Winnipeg to see shows and stuff." It was what people did. Mama had gone to lots of shows before she'd disappeared. It was one of her favourite things.

"We're not supposed to hitchhike."

"It's fine." At thirteen, Tia figured she was pretty good at telling nice from nasty. She would keep Tag safe.

"But why do we have to go at all?" Tag asked.

"You know why."

"Because of Scout."

"No, it's Cathy. She could have said yes. The lodge is huge."

A dog that big belongs in a zoo, not a house. Cathy had said.

Yeah, right, Tia thought. *Exaggerate much?* But Cathy had insisted the dog should go to the animal rescue centre. Remembering Cathy's words, and the argument that followed, made Tia's blood boil all over again.

But he needs a home, just like Tag and I did.

You and Tag are people.

So what? It's not like you don't have space.

I'm sorry, Tia, but the answer is no. I won't change my mind on this.

"He's just a dog," Tag said.

"How are you even my brother?"

Tia loved her brother with everything in her, but they were polar opposites in terms of personality. Tia was more like Mama—adventurous, willing to take a chance on things, while Tag was cautious. Maybe his nature came from their father. Daddy had died when Tag was a baby and Tia was five. Her memories of him were dim, but at least she had a few. More than Tag.

A gust of icy wind stole her breath, pushing her back. It was almost April, but the warmth of spring so recently arrived with early buds and sun kisses had disappeared like a promise it couldn't keep. Tia tucked her chin into her jacket collar, moving quickly. She was in a hurry to get some distance from Cathy and Bob's, the latest in a string of foster care placements.

"You'll love the Magnussons," their caseworker, Jamie, had said as she dropped them off one week and two days ago. She'd said the same thing about the other four homes Tia and Tag had been placed in over the past two and a half months, none of which had worked out.

As always, they'd carried their belongings in garbage bags. Kids in foster care didn't get suitcases. But garbage bags would make them stand out in this town, which would get them stopped before they'd hardly made a start.

When they'd left the house with Scout, fake mom and dad hadn't even noticed they were wearing their school backpacks. *It's not stealing*, Tia told herself. Cathy and Bob had said they were theirs to keep. But instead of notebooks, inside they each carried a toothbrush, extra socks and underwear, two shirts.

Jamie had promised the Magnussons' place would be different, and on the surface, it was. The home was in the country next to Lake Winnipeg but still close enough to the small town of Gimli that they could walk there if they didn't mind a short hike. Cathy and Bob ran a tourist lodge called the Great Blue Haven. Guests stayed in cabins nestled along Lake Winnipeg, while the family lived in the main house, serving up breakfasts in a quaint tearoom.

Oh, Cathy and Bob acted nice enough, but Tia knew it wouldn't last. It never did.

The Magnussons hadn't yelled at them or hit them or anything like that, but there was something about Cathy that got under Tia's skin. Apart from when she was saying "no," she was way too nice, like over the top, like a TV version of a mother. Tia couldn't figure her out. It wasn't like she was kid-starved or anything—Cathy and Bob already had young twin daughters, Summer and Daye.

Tia shivered and wished she'd thought to wear her sweater underneath her jacket.

"How much longer, Tia?"

"I'm not sure."

"C'mon, let's just go back. It wasn't so bad there. I liked it. Better than running away."

"We're not running *away*, we're running *to*. It's different. Besides, Uncle Richard is in Winnipeg. He's rich. He'll help us."

"He's not really our uncle."

"He said we could call him that."

"How do you know he's rich?"

"He lives in a hotel, doesn't he? That probably means he owns it."

"But we don't even know his last name," Tag argued. "Why can't we just call the hotels from here?"

"Because we can't," Tia snapped. She didn't need Tag pointing out that her plan wasn't that well thought out. "If we're there in person, they'll see we mean business."

"Who?"

"They! You know perfectly well who I mean! Anyway, Social Services knows about him, and they haven't done anything."

"Have too. Jamie said *they* couldn't find him."

"We have to find him ourselves. Besides, if the Magnussons really wanted us to stay, they would have said yes to Scout."

Okay, fine, maybe this wasn't really about Scout, but he *was* the final straw.

No, you can't take a break from school. No, you can't have food in your bedroom. No, you can't stay up past nine o'clock. No, Tag can't have extra applesauce in his lunch.

Tia's dark thoughts softened as the shaggy, blond dog in front of them glanced back over his shoulder, as if checking to see if they were still following. Mouth open, tongue lolling out one side over black lips, he looked like an Irish wolfhound with a little something else mixed in. He was a big dog, the biggest Tia had ever seen, but not the giant their new foster mother had made him out to be.

"How do you even know that's his name?" Tag asked.

"I don't know. He just looks like it—stop asking so many questions!"

"Sorry," Tag mumbled, sounding not sorry at all.

A slippery patch and a crazy dance to stay upright interrupted their bickering.

Tag grabbed hold, helping to steady her. "Are you okay?"

"Yeah. Weird weather."

Tia shivered again. From morning's first blink, grey skies had hung low and harried the land first with ice-cold drizzle, and then tiny snow pellets. There had even been the occasional rumble of thunder, though it had been faint, as if embarrassed. Now, as daylight began to fade, invisible fingers of ice snuck between folds of their outer wraps to replace warm spaces deep inside with something cold and hollow.

The last time the weather had been this strange was in October. The days had shortened like they always did, and leaves had all but blown from the trees. But one day after the morning frost had burned away, the sun got hotter and hotter, like a child stomping its foot in defiance. By evening, it was sweltering.

Long after Tag had gone to bed, Mama and Tia sat at the kitchen table, sipping iced peppermint tea. Mama moved to the open, night-darkened window and paused there, her fingertips resting lightly on the latch, looking out, as if seeing beyond the street, the city, to someplace faraway. She stood there so long that Tia wondered if she'd forgotten about her. Then, in a singsong voice, Mama confided that sometimes she thought about just taking off, getting a new name and starting a new life. When Tia asked what her and Tag's new names would be, she came back to herself, giggled, and said they had no one to hide from.

It was nothing. Just a silly what-if, like a story you sometimes imagined yourself inside. Except that it had made Tia feel all fluttery. She hadn't felt safe.

After that, she'd felt the same way every day. The dull ache in her chest she woke with would go away when she saw Mama at the table sipping her coffee, but it would grow back through the day, like a lengthening shadow, until she rushed home and saw Mama was still there.

Then, in January, Mama disappeared, and the shadow had wrapped all around her.

It hadn't taken long for Tia to grow tired of the sympathetic looks in people's eyes, the ones that said she and Tag were orphans.

But they weren't.

You can't be an orphan when you still have a mother, Tia thought. *Even if you don't know where she is.*

Tia bit her lip. She knew Tag liked Cathy and Bob, and she was taking him away anyway. It was for the best. No matter how nice they acted, they weren't family. Tia and Tag would never truly fit.

Maybe taking off was impulsive, but it didn't matter. All Tia knew was that she couldn't stay another minute at the Magnussons, and there was no way she'd leave Tag behind. Not ever. Abandoning people who love you was about the worst thing a person could ever do. That wasn't Tia.

And it wasn't Mama, either.

It couldn't be.

If she let herself think that, even for a second, she was afraid she'd forget how to breathe.

"Tia," Tag whimpered, touching her hand. He'd stopped in front of a wrought iron gate at the side of the road. It was an entrance to a small cemetery—one of those private family ones that dotted the countryside, abandoned and overgrown. Tag had always been terrified of cemeteries. Tia had no idea why. Maybe he'd seen some spooky movie, or maybe someone had told him a scary story. Whatever the reason, Tia had learned not to push or tease him. It only upset him more. Instead, she held his hand. As long as she stayed quiet, he'd calm.

Big, soft flakes of snow had begun to fall, insulating them, muffling any sound they might have heard from the highway, which wasn't too far away. Still, this road was little more than a lane, and as it disappeared around the next bend, poplar, aspen and spruce crowded the edges of it, reaching skyward. It was like the entrance to another world far from home.

Tia shook her head, breaking the spell. "Come on, let's keep moving."

All at once, there was a commotion from around the bend.

"Holy!" Tag cried.

Tia spun around as if an electric jolt had shocked her body. When she saw what had caused Tag to cry out, she froze.

Chapter Two

Like something from a dream, a small herd of horses came at them in an odd, running sort of walk, surrounding them, moving around them. Tag screamed, causing one to rear up in front of them.

Heart pounding, Tia wrapped her brother in her arms, shielding him. Amid the sounds of hooves clattering against gravel and the snorting and whinnying of the horses, she heard a dog barking. "Scout!" she called, fearful the dog would be stepped on, or would frighten the beasts even more.

The world became a swirl of colour—brown, black, cream, grey and white. The horses passed so close on either side that Tia could breathe in their warmth. She felt like a rock in river rapids and hoped with everything in her that this living stream wouldn't knock them down and trample them.

As suddenly as it had begun, it was over.

Tia let go of Tag and watched, expecting to see the horses disappear around the corner. Instead, they'd stopped and were now watching her with bold, intelligent eyes.

They were eight sturdy-looking animals, not as tall as most horses Tia had seen, but not as small as the ponies she'd fed handfuls of clover to at the summer fair in Winnipeg. The way they held their sculpted heads and curved their necks gave them a regal air. Their manes and forelocks were thick and luxurious. A chocolate-brown horse near the front shook its head, starting a chain reaction in three others.

After a moment, the herd settled and stood quiet. Their breath, which rose in white puffs, was sweet-scented, reminding Tia of summer fields. With their round bellies and shaggy, double-sided manes, they looked like something out of a storybook. She half expected small men with beards and giant double-sided axes to emerge from the trees.

Scout gave a small yip and emerged from behind the herd, looking at Tia and wagging his tail. A black and white horse standing slightly off to one side snorted and tapped the ground with a hoof, as if growing impatient, but Tia's eyes were drawn to the brown horse standing front and centre. It was heavier than the others, wide-bellied with four white stockings and a black mane and tail—except for a white splotch on its mane, which looked as if someone had dropped paint on it. Its eyes were big and soft, and it stared at Tia as if waiting for her to do something. But what?

"What's going on?" Tag whispered.

"They must have got loose from somewhere," Tia said, glancing back toward where the herd had first appeared. No help from tracks—the snow melted soon after it hit the road. Tia took a breath and made a decision. She stepped forward toward the centre horse.

"No, Tia, wait! What if it bites?"

Tia ignored her brother and took another step. Then another. Animals of all kinds had always liked her: cats, dogs, hamsters, even a baby fox she'd found behind the small house in the country they'd lived in for a while two years back. Tia had used baby bottles she'd snuck from the school daycare to nurse it until it was old enough to run away.

They'd only lived in that house for one spring and summer, just before they'd moved to Winnipeg, but of all the places they'd lived since Tag was born, it had been Tia's favorite. Mama liked it too but decided they couldn't stay there on account of there being no jobs in the nearby town.

It'd been hard moving around so much, having to make new friends, but there were always animals around, mostly dogs and cats chasing frisbees in parks or slinking down alleys. It was like they knew her, all the way to the inside of her, and would always stop and say hello. Animals never expected her to be anyone other than exactly who she was.

Horses, however, she'd only ever seen from a distance and read about in books. Something in her heart opened wide as she took in the ones in front of her, coats glistening, sweat steaming from their backs. After sniffing the air, the chocolate centre horse, which she could now see was a mare, stretched her neck, reaching toward her with her nose.

Focussing on the brown mare, Tia turned her body so that she looked less threatening. She didn't know how she knew to do that, but it felt right. If she was facing full on, an animal's instincts might read that as her being ready to chase—or attack.

Tia took a calming breath and willed it down though her body all the way to her toes. Removing one mitten, she held out her hand, palm up, fingers spread wide. The horse immediately thrust her nose into it. "I think she's looking for treats," Tia said, giggling as the horse licked her palm.

"What kind of horses are they?" Tag asked.

"How should I know?"

"They're kind of small."

The black-and-white horse pawed the ground and snorted.

Tag jumped. "But in a good way!"

Another horse, this one the colour of oatmeal with a white stripe down its nose, nudged Tia's arm, as if jealous for attention. She stroked its shoulder and craned her neck, trying to see beyond the horses. There was a fence tucked up against the trees, just beyond the ditch.

"I bet if we get them moving back up the road, we'll find an open gate somewhere," Tia said.

"How are we going to do that?" Tag asked, standing straight as a board, hand out for the sniffing horses.

"I'm not sure." Tia began gently pushing the mare back up the road the way the herd had come. "Move!" she cried. "Move!"

The black-and-white horse, still off to the side, squealed and spun in a circle. The others tossed their heads and snorted. Tag fell back again, looking fearful. Abruptly, Scout barked and began darting back and forth behind the horses, letting out sharp yips.

"Look at Scout!" Tia cried. "He knows what to do." Trying again, she looped an arm over the mare's neck and pushed her in the direction she wanted the horses to go.

With Scout barking and darting behind them, the herd apparently decided moving wasn't such a bad idea. Soon they were all heading back around the curve in the road, where, sure enough, there was an open gate. Tia put her hand against the mare's neck to guide her, and the mare walked through without protest. The other horses followed, except for two who looked like they might try and make a break for it. Scout convinced them otherwise.

"What if that's not their place?" Tag asked as they closed the gate.

Tia shrugged and peered into the surrounding woods. "There must be a farm around here somewhere. Let's look."

"What about Winnipeg and Richard?"

"We're still going," Tia said, frowning.

"Or we could just stay here. What kind of a person lives in a hotel, even if they do own it?" Tag muttered.

Tia didn't answer. In truth, she didn't know, but the way Mama talked about him, blue eyes flashing as she flung a swath of hair over her shoulder, made Richard seem like a pretty big deal.

"I think he's a good man at heart," Mama had said, which struck Tia as odd. Did that mean a person could be good in their heart but not on the outside? Richard's outside seemed okay to her. She wished with everything in her that she'd asked Mama what she meant, as that was one of the last things she'd said before she'd disappeared.

At first, Tia hadn't worried. Mama knew Tia was old enough to look after things. She'd told her so. And last fall, just before Mama started her new waitressing job, she'd promised Tia that even though sometimes she was away longer than she planned, maybe even overnight, she would always be back before they ran out of peanut butter.

Mama had kept that promise, until this last time.

Tia had made the peanut butter last as long as she could—that and anything else she could turn into a meal. But eventually, they'd turned to the school breakfast program. Tia knew there would be questions, but they'd had no choice. Then the stupid principal called Social Services. No one had listened when Tia insisted her mother would be back.

Tia came up with her plan to go to Winnipeg right after Cathy had said no to keeping Scout. Just like that, it had become her mantra: First, they'd find Richard, and then, they'd find Mama.

First Richard, then Mama, first Richard, then Mama.

"Come on, we have to tell someone about the horses." She jogged up the road as Tag and Scout kept pace beside her. The snow was falling heavier now, as if someone had taken a giant box of soap flakes and shaken it over their heads.

As they rounded the bend past the cemetery, something crashed out from the bush in front of them.

Startled, Tia grabbed hold of Tag and drew him close.

"Hold on!" the something said. "I didn't mean to scare you." As he pulled off a his red-and-green plaid jacket hood, Tia saw a curly grey beard first, then twinkling eyes and a red knit cap. The old man wore dirty yellow work gloves and carried what looked like a game of cat's cradle, made of nylon rope instead of string. Scout ran over to him, wagging his tail.

"Oh, hey there, fella! What's your name?"

Tag pulled away from Tia. "That's Scout—"

"Shush," Tia said, taking Tag's hand and speaking into his ear. "He's a stranger."

"Scout likes him."

Tia squeezed Tag's hand. "We weren't scared. You just surprised us."

"I was scared," Tag said.

Tia squeezed his hand again.

"Hey, ow!"

The man's brows smashed together. "Are you two okay? Are you lost? I haven't seen you around."

"Not lost," Tia said.

Tag pulled his hand out of Tia's. "We're staying near here. I'm Tag."

"Tag!"

The man smiled all the way to his eyes. "You can call me Grandpa Bebe," he said. "Say, you haven't seen some horses around here, have you?"

"Maybe." Tia hedged, then relented. "Yes. There was an open gate back around the corner. We put them in there."

"All by yourselves?"

Tia nodded toward the dog. "Scout helped." Her stranger-danger apprehension was melting away. The man looked like a friendly, slightly greyer cousin to jolly old St. Nick. Plus, she was pretty sure she and Tag could outrun him if they felt the need.

"Your dog?" Grandpa Bebe asked, rubbing behind Scout's ears.

"Not exactly."

"Sounds like a story in there, but that place you put my horses isn't my property. Let's go get those silly buttheads."

"I thought they were horses," Tag quipped.

Grandpa Bebe grinned. "I love them to bits, but if there's trouble to get into, they'll find it!"

They hurried along the lane, the man quick and sure of foot on the slippery roads. Around the corner, they spotted the herd. The horses hadn't moved from where Tia and Tag had left them and watched quietly from behind the gate. Tia leaned over the fence as Grandpa Bebe opened the gate and pushed himself between the horses.

The black-and-white horse nickered, tossing his head.

"Hello, Garri, my old friend," the man greeted the animal. "Were you waiting for me to find you?"

As if to answer, the horse—Garri—neighed.

The chocolate mare moved toward Tia, lifted her nose to Tia's face, sniffed and blowed, as if exchanging breath.

"Well, I'll be," Grandpa Bebe said. "I've never seen Disa do that."

Tia lifted her hand, hesitated, then with a feather touch, stroked the mare's nose. "Hello, Disa," she whispered.

"Will you help me get them up the road?" he asked Tia.

"We don't know much about horses," she said.

"Actually, we don't know anything about horses," Tag said.

The man laughed. "No matter. Disa is the boss mare. They'll follow her. With your help—and Scout's—we'll have them home in no time." He took the nylon halter he'd been carrying and slipped it over Disa's head. "Will you take her?" he asked Tia.

This was crazy. Was he actually handing her a rope to lead a real, live horse, as if she had an actual clue what to do with it? Instead of pinching herself, she bit her lip. She was definitely not dreaming. She gulped. "Where?"

"Just around the bend."

The mare's eyes were deep brown, and she looked, unblinking, at Tia. Something sparked deep in her chest, a feeling, as clear as if spoken out loud: *trust.* She felt something warm wash through her. "Okay," she said, taking the rope.

"Great! Hold the extra rope folded like this." He flattened the loops and placed them in her hand. "Never let it get wrapped around your hand in case the horse gets frightened and bolts. Better to let her get away than for you to get dragged."

"Will that happen?" Tia asked, a twinge of fear in her belly.

The man winked. "Not likely. Disa is as steady as they come. You go ahead. This young man and I will bring up the rear."

Carefully taking the lead rope, Tia whispered to the mare. "I won't hurt you, girl. You don't hurt me either, okay?" The horse's slow blink calmed her. She turned and started back up the road, calling over her shoulder. "How far?"

"I'll let you know when to turn!" Grandpa Bebe called after her. She watched him lean toward Tag, exchange a few words she couldn't hear. "Thanks, Tia!" he called.

She scowled at Tag, who grinned and shrugged. Helping out was one thing, but he shouldn't have told her name. That was hers to give, and she would rather have kept that to herself. Tag had never been as good as Tia at keeping quiet.

Oh well. What was that saying? Once the cat was out of the bag, you couldn't put it back, or something like that.

Tia was lulled by the rhythm of walking and falling snow. The day had taken a turn that felt magical. As Disa followed her lead, she imagined herself in another life, a cowgirl on a ranch. Maybe rich Uncle Richard also had a place in the country with horses. Maybe once Tia and Tag found him, and then Mama, they could all live there together.

Tia was so lost in her daydream that she almost missed the wooden signpost to her right. Hanging from the post was a sign that read "Ice Pony Ranch and Animal Rescue Centre."

"Turn here," Grandpa Bebe said.

You've got to be kidding me, Tia thought as she turned Disa up the path. This was the place Cathy had wanted her to bring Scout. And here they were. It felt like the heavy hand of doom. Or fate. Or Cathy. All the same thing.

No. They'd bring in the horses and be on their way.

Glancing behind, she saw the man stepping spryly beside the small herd, waving his arms and causing the horses to turn. The black-and-white horse gave a small back kick, as if in protest, but still moved to where Grandpa Bebe wanted him to go.

Poplar, pine and birch trees crowded even closer to the road now. As Tia rounded the bend, the trees fell behind her, and she was suddenly in the wide-open space that was Ice Pony Ranch.

Chapter Three

The feeling that welled up inside of Tia at the sight of Ice Pony Ranch was like longing and joy and comfort all mixed up together. It was like stepping into a painting, one where you knew that at any second, someone might come down the lane or a stag might leap from the brush and bound across the meadow. Perfection existed in that moment just before, when anything could happen.

A long driveway divided two sides of a wide meadow surrounded by a white painted fence. There were additional paddocks within the meadow, each one with small wooden shelters and hay bins. At the end of the drive, there were three buildings: a sky-blue bungalow to one side, a red barn to the other, and, in the middle, a T-shaped building in a darker shade of blue with a sign that said, "Shelter."

As Tia led the small herd up the drive, Grandpa Bebe moved ahead of her and opened a big, wooden gate. He took Disa from her and led the mare inside. The other horses followed, shaking their heads, whickering, and snorting.

"Thanks for your help," Grandpa Bebe said, closing the gate behind him.

Tag looked at the T-shaped building. "Tia, isn't this where Cathy told you to bring Scout?"

"Cathy?" Grandpa Bebe asked.

"She's our foster mom."

"Tag!"

"What?"

She turned back to Grandpa Bebe. "Sorry if my brother talked your ear off."

"Not at all. I've known Cathy and Bob for years. They're good people."

Tia and Tag climbed on the slats of the wooden fence to watch. As Grandpa Bebe moved amongst the horses, stroking them, talking to them, Tia whispered to Tag. "Tag, he's a stranger. You shouldn't be telling him stuff."

"But he's nice," Tag whispered back. "And we know his name. And he knows Cathy and Bob."

Tia tried, and failed, to hold back a grin. "You have no idea how lucky you are to have me looking after you."

"I know," Tag said, looking serious.

Grandpa walked and rubbed the horse's necks and ears. "Gelmir, how are you today, my old friend?" He stopped at a grey horse. "Björn, how's your leg today, buddy?" He tapped behind Björn's hoof. The horse lifted his foot, and Grandpa Bebe caught hold and examined his leg.

"Those are weird names," Tag said.

"They're Icelandic," Grandpa Bebe explained. "And these are Icelandic Horses—a very old breed from a land far from here." His eyes took on a faraway look, as if he was actually seeing it. "They're very special."

"I think all horses are special," Tia said.

"You like horses?" Grandpa Bebe asked.

Tia shrugged. "I like all animals."

"She's crazy about them," Tag said.

"Well, in that case, you'll like the shelter. Want to come in and warm up? They love visitors."

"Can we?" Tag asked. "I'm cold."

She glanced at Scout, who wagged his tail. *He knows Cathy and Bob*, the dog seemed to be reassuring her. She looked back at her brother, his pleading, hopeful look melting her.

"I guess, Tia said." But just for a minute."

Grandpa Bebe led them past the barn to the middle building. Up close, Tia saw a narrow front deck that ran the whole length of the structure. The building was joined to the barn through a covered walkway. Beside the door, there was a half rain barrel with straw sticking out of it. A goat was nibbling from it, but scooted away as they approached. A moment later, it stuck its head back around the corner of the building and bleated at them.

"Relax, Horatio!" He cooed, then turned back to Tia and Tag. "He's a little shy with new folks." He pulled open the front door. "Come on in!"

Inside, there was a small space that looked like an office with a small desk and a computer. Along the back wall, there was a counter with a giant cage on top. The cage was empty, the door left open. The tangy smell of pine cleaner was strong but not unpleasant.

Dogs from somewhere in the building must have heard them, because one barked, followed by another. Soon there was a whole chorus of barking dogs. To Tia, it sounded like music. She'd always wanted a pet of her own, especially a dog. Mama had said it wasn't possible, that moving so often wouldn't be fair to an animal. When Scout had turned up on the Magnussons' doorstep, he was like a gift from the universe. But nothing ever turned out the way Tia hoped.

As if on cue, the barking died away to a few yips, then nothing. "What lives in there?" Tia asked, pointing to the cage.

"That would be Raphael, our resident raven," Grandpa Bebe explained. "But he's out with Jennifer right now."

"Jennifer?"

"My daughter. She's the owner of this ranch. I only work here," he said, winking. "Which would you like to see first, cats or dogs?"

"I don't know. It doesn't matter."

"Dogs it is then! Better have your dog wait in the office for now. No point in getting the others all excited."

He led them through a red door at the back of the office which opened to a small room with a washtub against one wall and a hand-held sprayer hooked on the wall just above.

"Everyone gets a bath—first, when they get here, then once a week, more often if they need it," Grandpa Bebe said. "Even the cats."

There were three additional doors leading from the washing room: one at the back, with a brown, bristly looking doormat in front of it—Tia guessed that led outdoors—one to the left, and one to the right. Those doors were helpfully labeled, one with the word *DOGS* and the other with the word *CATS*.

The dogs must have heard Grandpa Bebe's voice, because the excited yipping started up again. The old man grinned and opened the door, motioning for Tia go ahead of him.

Inside was a large space. Caged dog runs holding dogs of all shapes and sizes lined one wall. Each run had a soft-looking blanket and bed inside and a small latched door at the back. Tia counted seven dogs in all. Most looked like some sort of shepherd or husky mix, but there were two smaller dogs, one of them not even the size of a loaf of bread. Tia recognized it as a Chihuahua.

"There are outdoor runs for each of them," Grandpa Bebe said. "Plus, we take them out for walks and playtime when we can."

Tia stopped by the Chihuahua. It was shaking and cowering in the back corner of its cage.

"We're pretty sure that fella has been abused," Grandpa Bebe told her. "He's been here for a week, but he won't let anyone near him."

"Can I try?" Tia asked.

Grandpa Bebe pooched out his lips. "Well ..." He looked again at the Chihuahua. Finally, he nodded. "I don't see why not. He's not an aggressive dog, but if he gets snappy, respect his space."

Tia opened the door and sat down just inside the dog run. As Grandpa Bebe and Tag moved off to look at the other orphaned animals, Tia spoke softly to the small dog. She imagined a blanket of calm coming down over them. It was insulating, and soon the sounds of Tag, Grandpa Bebe, and the other dogs fell away. She willed him to trust her, to feel her care. Seconds ticked. Nearly a minute, maybe longer. Finally, as if suddenly offering up a telepathic "okay," the Chihuahua took tentative steps toward her.

When Grandpa Bebe and Tag returned, the Chihuahua was sitting on Tia's lap, quivering and licking her chin. She giggled and softly stroked his back.

"Well, I'll be," Grandpa Bebe said. "You have a gift, young lady."

Reluctantly, Tia gave the little dog a final pet. She could see hope shining from his eyes. It reminded her of how Tag looked at her as he played with the Magnussons' twin daughters. She turned quickly to Grandpa Bebe. "Where next?"

"Want to see the cats?"

"Of course!"

Grandpa Bebe led them back through to the washing room and into the cat shelter. It was like something out of a movie. There were wire box kennels stacked against one wall, and in the center of the room, there was a wide-open area with a miniature indoor tree house of sorts. Much of it was covered in carpet, and there were cats of all sizes and colours climbing all over it.

"We get a lot of cats," Grandpa Bebe explained. "Some of them are here for a long time. We just want to make it nice for them."

"No one wants them?" Tag asked.

Tia curled her fingertips into her palm, stifling an urge to smooth the creases in her brother's forehead. She wanted to hug him, remind him he wasn't a cat. *She* wanted him. Until Mama got back, it was her job to make sure he felt safe and loved.

"There are so many of them," Tia said. "They look pretty happy."

Grandpa Bebe chuckled. "They are. Jennifer and I make sure they get plenty of attention. Probably not as much as they like, but we do what we can."

As they reentered the washing room, a woman's voice could be heard coming from the front office.

"Speaking of Jennifer ...." Grandpa Bebe opened the door to a woman, now seated at the desk, her wavy hair as black as the raven perched next to her. "Tia, Tag, this is my daughter, Jennifer."

Jennifer smiled, her eyes crinkling like Grandpa Bebe's, but with fewer lines.

Scout looked settled and happy on a mat by the front door. Tia was pretty sure that mat hadn't been there when they'd arrived.

"Jennifer, this is Tia and Tag," Grandpa Bebe said. "They helped me round up our wandering horses."

"Hello, Tia and Tag. Thank you so much for your help! Has my dad been giving you a tour?"

Tia nodded. "Yes. This place is so wonderful!" The truth of it brought a lump to her throat. If she were a stray animal, this would be a cool place to live. It made her feel good to see the animals happy, especially Scout.

As if he could read her mind, Scout got up from his resting place and licked Tia's hand.

"Is this your dog?" Jennifer asked. "I was wondering where he came from."

"We found him," Tag said. "But Cathy said we can't keep him. That's why we were going to Winnipeg."

Tia glared at him. "Tag, shush!"

Jennifer and Grandpa Bebe stared at her, eyes like lasers. She turned her attention to her thumb and a hangnail. It was so quiet, she could hear the clicking of the baseboard heaters. Or maybe that was Raphael's beak.

"Cathy?" Jennifer asked. "As in Cathy and Bob Magnusson?"

"They're our new parents," Tag said.

Tia shot him a look. "Foster parents, Tag. Just temporary." She turned back to Grandpa Bebe and Jennifer. "Just until our mom comes back."

Jennifer and Grandpa Bebe exchanged a glance, and again the room fell silent.

Grandpa Bebe cleared his throat. "Winnipeg! That's a long way to go, especially when we've got a perfectly good place for dogs right here."

Tia laughed, but it sounded fake even to her. "We weren't really going to Winnipeg."

"We weren't?" Tag asked.

"I was just trying to figure things out, Tag." She rubbed Scout behind his ear. "We couldn't just leave him. He's my friend."

"Could you leave him here just for tonight?" Jennifer asked. "The way this snow is coming down, it would be nice for him to be somewhere warm and dry."

Tia looked out the window at the darkening sky, and her heart sank. She knew the snow wouldn't last long—it would probably melt in the next day or so—but she also knew that, at least for now, they wouldn't be hitching a ride anywhere.

"I have another idea," Grandpa Bebe said. He turned to his daughter. "Jennifer, you know how we haven't been able to get near that little Chihuahua?"

Jennifer nodded.

"Tia here had him sitting on her lap in a matter of minutes."

"Really?" Jennifer looked at Tia, obviously impressed. "We've been trying with him all week."

"She has a natural way with animals. Disa went right to her."

Jennifer smiled at Tia. "We have been a little short-handed around here. What do you say, Tia? Can you spare a little time?"

"For what?" It felt like the room was tilting. She touched the wall to make sure she didn't slip. "You mean, like ... a job? I've never had a job before. Outside of babysitting, I mean."

"Would you like one?" Jennifer asked.

Tia pinched herself to see if this was real, then she pinched herself harder. "What would I do?"

"Cleaning kennels, playing with the animals, basically making them happy and comfortable."

"What about the horses?"

Grandpa Bebe chuckled. "One step at a time. This is where we need you most. And, you can hang out with Scout while you are here."

Scout was bright-eyed, tail wagging. Everything about him beaming, "Yes!" Winnipeg suddenly felt far away. It hadn't been a very good plan, anyway. This might give her time to think of something better. "I'd like that, thanks."

A crunch of tires on gravel drew their attention. Tag ran to the window as doors slammed. The excited chatter of small children could be heard.

"It's Cathy and Bob," Tag cried. "And the twins!"

Tia scowled at Grandpa Bebe. He must have called them when he and Tag left Tia with the Chihuahua. Of course he did, thanks to her blabbermouth brother.

Grandpa Bebe opened the door to a wide-shouldered man followed by a woman and two children, who pushed past into the office, giggling.

"Hi, guys!" Bob said. "Uh, sorry about the chaos. Kids wanted to come."

"It's happy chaos, Bob," Grandpa Bebe said. "Best kind." His knees crackled as he knelt in front of the twins. "Summer, Daye, where's my hug?" They leapt into his arms, still giggling.

Bob ruffled Tag's hair. "How you doing, buddy?"

Cathy moved toward Tia. "We were worried."

Tia squared her shoulders, felt annoyance rise. "We were fine."

Cathy opened her mouth as if to respond, then looked away.

Bob pulled off his wool cap and gloves. His hands were oily, as if he'd been holding a piece of machinery. He must have been working in the shed. "Cathy was getting worried, with the snow and all."

"We were both worried," Cathy corrected.

He grinned. "That's right. Anyway, glad you're both okay."

"Can we play with the kitties?" Summer asked Grandpa Bebe.

"Kitties!" Daye echoed, jumping up and down.

Using the desk as anchor, Grandpa Bebe pulled himself back upright, turned to Cathy and Bob, "That okay with you?"

Cathy glanced at Tia. "Okay, but not for long."

"Follow me, girls. I'll get you settled in the playroom. Tag, you want to join us?"

Tag nodded and clasped hands with Summer and Day.

"I'll come too," Bob said, following them through the door.

As the door closed, the chattering and giggling faded, and Tia could once again hear the clicking of the baseboard heaters. Definitely not Raphael's beak.

Tia braced herself for a scolding.

Cathy look another step toward her. "Tia, I—"

"I got a job," Tia blurted.

"Oh." That stopped her. Cathy looked from Tia to Jennifer. "A job?"

Jennifer smiled. "Why don't I get us some coffee?"

Chapter Four

To anyone else, the rustic lodge kitchen with its home-crafted touches would be cheery, but as Tia sat at the table shaking cereal into her bowl, she sussed tension in the set of Cathy's shoulders. Warily, she watched as Cathy took last night's plates from the dishwasher and placed them, one by one, in the cupboard.

Finally, she turned. "I'm just not sure about this, Tia."

"About what?" Tia had already guessed what, but wanted Cathy to say it. No way was she going to make things easier for her.

"The animal shelter. The job. Bob and I talked about it more last night, and it's just not a good idea. For us. For all of us. As a family."

Tia felt her inner storm clouds gather. "We are not a family."

"We're ..." Cathy faltered. "Okay, that's not the point."

"You told Grandpa Bebe and Jennifer it sounded fine."

"I know, but—Look, this doesn't have to be an argument. I'm just concerned."

"Concerned."

"Yes."

"Then why did you tell Grandpa Bebe and Jennifer it was okay if you didn't mean it. Were you lying?"

Cathy turned her head to the side as if struck. She took a deep breath, closed the cupboard door, and joined Tia at the table.

With the back of her spoon, Tia crushed her cereal against the side of the bowl. This was just another terrible placement.

"Tia, I—" Cathy took another breath. "Look, I understand why you're upset. But this isn't just about you. It's about all of us."

Tia put her spoon down. "So it's because you care."

"Yes. I don't want you to take on too much when everything here is so new to you." Cathy placed a hand over hers. "And even though we are not a family by birth or adoption, we are still connected by caring. I'd like us to have a little time to bond."

Tia jerked her hand away. "What's the point? Temporary, remember? My mother is coming back."

Cathy turned her head away, but not quick enough to hide her frustration. Tia had been watching for it. That, and more. At least Cathy wasn't yelling. At their last placement, there would have been yelling.

"But Scout is there," Tia said.

"Scout?"

"The dog you wouldn't let us keep. Maybe if you liked animals you'd get it."

"I like animals," Cathy said. "For goodness sake, Tia. It's not that I didn't like the dog, it's just that we have our hands full running this lodge right now."

Tia bit back a "*Whatever!*" and searched the bottom of her cereal bowl for inspiration. There was one more thing she could try. If she said this next part just right ... "But, Scout is over there, and the horses, and they need help and"—she snuck a sly glance at Cathy—"and helping animals is something that I'm good at. I'm not good at much."

The pain that flashed in Cathy's eyes startled Tia. *Focus, Tia*, she told herself. *Don't feel bad. Don't cave. Besides, it isn't a lie. Not exactly.*

After six loud ticks of the clock on the wall, Cathy sighed.

It was what she was waiting for. Tia mustered her most hopeful, pleading, pitiful look. At least, she hoped that was how it came across. "Please?"

Cathy moved back over to the counter and poured herself a coffee. Finally, she turned. "You should think about joining the debating club at school, Tia."

Seriously? She hadn't expected Cathy to give in so easily. "Is that a yes?"

Cathy studied her. "Just give me today to think about it, okay? I really want us to work as a family."

"But it's Saturday." If she pushed just a little harder, she could be at the shelter in ten minutes!

"Give me today," Cathy repeated.

Tia held Cathy's gaze. It was firm and unyielding.

"Fine," Tia muttered. She put her cereal bowl in the now empty dishwasher, her mind still working furiously. It was going to take more than words to make this happen. It bugged her that Cathy had already said yes once. The fact that she'd gone back on her word said a lot about her, and none of it good.

It didn't matter. Tia was ready for the challenge.

Mama had always said actions spoke louder than words. If she wanted Cathy to say yes, Tia would have to show Cathy bonding. She would bond the heck out of this day, until there was no way Cathy could say no.

One day. No problem. She just needed to give a little more than she had been. Be cooperative and stuff.

After rinsing dishes collected from the lodge guests, she loaded the dishwasher while Cathy pounded bread dough in a big bowl. When Cathy asked her to wipe the dining room tables, instead of groaning and rolling her eyes as she usually did, she nodded, and said, "Of course."

Not too much, she told herself. *Don't let Cathy think this is fake—or a way to control you.*

No one would do that. Not ever. Tia was her own person. Mama had always let her be independent, encouraged it even. When Tia had wanted to go to her first day of kindergarten wearing her sweater inside out, which was way more interesting, Mama had let her. And when Tia had come home from school three days later saying the kids were mean and she wanted to quit, Mama had let her do that too. She'd warned her, however, that when she decided to go back, and Mama assured her she would, she would not lie and write a note to say that Tia had been sick. Instead, Tia would have to stand up and tell the truth.

And so she did, which didn't help her situation with her classmates. Even little kids could be cruel.

Thankfully, Mama had moved them to another part of the city a few months later, and Tia had started kindergarten afresh, this time with her sweater right side out. She was nothing if not adaptable.

Tia washed the sticky bread dough from her hands and hung the apron Cathy insisted she wear on a hook by the door. She found Cathy sweeping the back deck, the twins bundled in matching jackets and hats nearby, playing with cups and sandcastle shovels. "Want me to look after Summer and Daye?" she asked.

Cathy looked up at her as if startled. "No, that's fine, Tia. But if you're looking for something to do, we just had a guest check out of cabin two. Will you gather the linens?"

"Sure, of course." She saved her scowl until she was around the corner.

She had finished her babysitting course and she'd been looking after Tag since almost forever, whether Mama had been around or not. But, no, Cathy wouldn't dare trust a foster kid to care for her precious babies.

After dumping the linens in the laundry room, Tia ducked into the hallway-nook-turned-office where there was a computer for guests, and waited, trying not to fidget, while one of their departing guests—a children's book author who had been there to "soak up the quiet and finish some final chapters"—printed out her airline boarding passes.

With a goodbye and a promise to read the book once it came out, Tia slipped into the chair and began her research. When Cathy said yes—again—to Ice Pony Ranch, Tia wanted to be ready. She was comfortable around cats and dogs, but needed to learn more about horses. Icelandic horses, to be specific. This would be her first real job, and she wanted to be ready to pitch in anywhere she was needed.

If you are going to do a job, do it better than anyone else. Mama hadn't given her that advice. No one had. It was just something Tia knew.

She typed "Icelandic Horse" into a search engine, and before long her mind was feasting on photos and information. She learned that "Iceys" were smart, loved people, and were typically very strong and healthy. They also had two special extra gaits besides walking, trotting and galloping, which was most horses could do. One was called the "flying pace." The other, called the "tolt," was like a smooth, running walk.

Tia thought back to when she'd first seen the horses pounding down the road, knees lifting high followed by a quick, downward step, but so level it was like they might carry a bowl of soup on their backs without spilling a drop. That was probably what they'd been doing then—tolting. The Icelandic horse might just be the most interesting breed ever. How cool that there were a bunch of them right here in Gimli. And how lucky she'd been invited to work with them. Okay, fine, the job was at the shelter, but Grandpa Bebe had hinted that she might also work with the horses.

It would be extra awful if Cathy said no.

A tug at her shirt made Tia jump. It was Summer. Her sister was right behind her, finger in nose, as always.

"Tia," Summer whimpered, looking nervous.

Alarm shot through her. She spun her chair and dropped to her knee in front of the child. "What's wrong?" Summer was a bold, loud preschooler. She didn't whimper.

Summer tipped her head to one side. "My ear hurts."

"Oh ... oh no!"

Not the right thing to say. It was as if she'd flipped a switch causing Summer to accelerate from whimper to wail in two seconds flat.

"It's okay, Summer!" She tried to sound reassuring, but it was hard to be soothing and comforting when she had to shout to be heard. She glanced up the hall. "Where's your mom?" Bob was probably working in the yard, but Cathy should be somewhere close.

"What happened?" she asked Daye.

"Da wocks," Daye said, looking unconcerned.

"Rocks?" Tia's hand flew to her sweater pocket. Two days ago, the sun was warm, snow had melted from the lake-shore, and Tia had collected a few small stones she thought were pretty. She'd shown them to the twins and explained she might make jewelry from them. They'd liked them and had wanted to see them again and again. When the snow had started falling again, Tia forgot about the stones. She pulled them out now and counted: one, two.

There should have been seven.

"These rocks?" Tia had to shout to be heard above Summer's cries.

"Da otha ones," Daye said.

"What other ones?" Tia asked.

"Not those ones."

It didn't make sense. Tia picked Summer up, cradling the screaming child against her shoulder.

Where was Cathy?

Clutching Summer, she raced down the hall and met Tag at the kitchen door. Behind him on the table, there was his hat, a screwdriver and what looked like an old radio with a panel removed.

"What's going on?"

"Find Cathy!"

As Tag dashed out, Tia saw one of the plastic cups the twins had been playing with sitting by the door. Inside, she saw what looked like her missing stones. Not the ones currently in her pocket. It was the "otha" ones—missing, now found.

All but one, which couldn't have been bigger than a pea.

"One of these rocks?" Tia asked Daye, shouting to be heard above Summer's wails.

"Not those," Daye said, looking at her like she was crazy. "The wock in hah eaya."

Kid logic.

Panic washed over Tia. She tipped Summer over her knee at an awkward angle and jiggled her body from knee to knee in hopes that the errant stone would fall out.

Rocks were not supposed to be in children's heads. What would happen if it didn't come out? Would Summer go deaf? Would it somehow go through to her brain and kill her?

As Cathy rushed in with Tag hot on her heels, Tia was shouting like a maniac: "Out! Out! Out!"

Cathy tossed a wet rag she'd been carrying on the counter and lifted a red-faced and wailing Summer from Tia's lap. "Hush, sweetness, hush." Her voice was quiet, but still easily heard.

After a moment, Summer's shrieks softened to a whimper with an occasional hiccup. Cathy turned to Tia, her face tight and unreadable. "What happened?"

"It wasn't my fault," Tia said, her voice small.

"Just tell me!"

"She took one of the rocks I found down by the lake," Tia rushed. "I think it's in her ear."

Instead of panicking, Cathy nodded as if this made total sense. "Have you got rocks in your head, my love?" she cooed.

Daye squealed with laughter. Summer gave a small, uncertain smile.

After setting Summer gently back on the floor, Cathy turned her head and peered inside her ear. "Not to worry," she said, her voice light and calm. "A pair of tweezers will take care of this toot sweet."

"Can you get it?" Summer whimpered.

Cathy smiled. "Wouldn't you rather have Dr. Butler take care of this, honey? He fixes up children all the time."

"He gave me medithin," Daye offered.

"Yes, he did, sweetie, and he'll take care of Summer too."

Tia watched and listened with a mixture of horror and awe. "Should I call the clinic?" she asked, anxious.

Cathy smiled as if she'd just offered to check movie listings. If it was an act for Summer's sake, it was very good. "Sure. Tell them what happened, and that we'll be there in ten minutes. Tag, will you ask Bob to get the van?"

Tag nodded and was off like a shot.

While Cathy bundled up Summer and Daye in boots, jackets, and mittens, Tia flipped through the phonebook, hands shaking. She accidentally tore a page. "Oh, man!" she cried.

When she glanced up, Cathy's mask had fallen slightly, her face now shadowed with a slight frown. "The number is on the fridge, Tia." She hustled the twins out the front door.

As Tia dialed the number, an echo of what had just happened settled in, along with the realization that Cathy would never trust her with the twins now. It was so unfair. It wasn't that she wanted so badly to babysit, but she hated being misjudged.

A moment later, Tag came back inside, shivering from the cold.

"What were you doing outside without your jacket?" Tia scolded, harsher than she should. Her emotions were all mixed up in a ball of something somewhere between panic and anger. She wasn't mad at Tag, though. She was mad at herself.

"I was on the porch."

"Still, not okay to—oh, hello?" Tia turned for focus back to the telephone. With the clinic receptionist on the line, she explained quickly what had happened and that Cathy was on her way.

Now that the urgency had passed, Tia couldn't help but notice that when push came to shove, Cathy had bundled her *real* family into the car, even though there was no need for Daye to go.

Whatever. She and Tag were used to being left behind.

◆

Tia was at the computer busily erasing all the notes she'd made about Icelandic horses when Cathy and Bob returned with the twins.

"All is well," Cathy said, dropping a pebble on the desk.

Tia snatched the stone and threw it in the trashcan. Cathy watched, but said nothing. Probably finding words to tell her the job was out.

Tia had screwed things up again. It hadn't even taken her the whole day. "I guess you're mad," she said.

Cathy raised her brows. "That Summer stuck something in her ear? Of course not. Kids will be kids, though I don't think she'll do that again."

Tia nodded. "That's good."

Cathy was still looking at her. If she wasn't here to blast Tia about Summer, why was she staring at her?

Maybe it was worse.

She felt her armpits begin to sweat and itch.

In the heat of the moment, when Cathy burst into the kitchen, Tia had Summer over her knee. It must have looked awful, even if Tia's intentions had been good. Cathy hadn't even asked her to explain.

This was it. Cathy and Bob were done with Tia and Tag.

Sure, she'd been ready to leave yesterday, but that had been her choice. And it hadn't been to another temporary home; it had been to find their mother. Different situation entirely.

Tia dropped her head and waited for the inevitable. At least she would have the satisfaction of hearing Fake Mom come clean about how she really felt. All of that talk about bonding was complete garbage. She didn't really care about Tia and Tag. She was just like everyone else.

Tia willed the butterflies and nausea brewing in her belly to stay put. She snuck a glance and saw Cathy was thinking hard about something. But when she finally opened her mouth to speak, the roaring in Tia's ears was so loud she almost didn't hear what came next.

"Not every day. Every two days at most. Family and homework must come first."

"Ah ... what?" Confusion swirled.

"Ice Pony Ranch," Cathy said. "You still want to work there, don't you?"

Chapter Five

"Good morning, Tia!" Grandpa Bebe said. "Let me officially welcome you to Ice Pony Ranch and Rescue Centre."

Tia grinned as she clasped Grandpa Bebe's offered hand in a firm handshake. "Am I late?" Puffing from running the whole way, she glanced at the clock. It was just past seven a.m. She couldn't remember the last time she'd been awake and moving so early on a Sunday. Cathy had insisted she eat breakfast before she left, and even though Tia had inhaled the pancake and eggs in about five seconds, it'd still felt like five seconds too long.

"Not at all." He immediately got to the business of showing her the feeding and cleaning schedule, then gave her a more in-depth tour than the one he'd given Friday evening. She learned where to find cleaning products, foods, medicines, and, most importantly, treats!

"Can I leave you to it?" Grandpa Bebe asked as they returned to the front office.

"Of course!"

"Great. I'll be in the barn if you have any questions, and Jennifer's in the house."

Tia set to work. Even though she was cleaning out smelly cat boxes and wet, soiled newspaper from the bottom of kennels, she couldn't remember the last time she'd felt happier.

Mid-morning, Tia decided to take a break and visit the horse paddocks between the barn and the larger fenced fields.

There were three: one for the geldings, one for the mares, and one more that was currently empty. Everywhere, there were muddy prints.

The sun had risen warm and bright, and the snow had melted away as if embarrassed, a seasonal mistake. She breathed in the scents of fresh green things and damp earth, then scanned the small herd of horses, hoping to spot Disa, the chocolate mare. She didn't see her, but after a few minutes, the black-and-white horse, Garri, wandered over, whickered then snuffled her shoulder as if he recognized her. Maybe it was because Tia had carrots in her pocket—just a few. She didn't want Cathy to complain that she was giving away all their groceries.

Tia sighed happily as she watched the horses. She hadn't forgotten about Richard and Winnipeg and looking for Mama, but Ice Pony Ranch would be a good place to spend time while she figured things out.

Grandpa Bebe appeared from around the corner. He twisted a coil of rope and slung it over his shoulder, "How's it going, Tia?"

"Good, I guess. No problems."

"Ready for some lunch?"

She nodded.

After sandwiches and cocoa in the house with Jennifer, Tia watched Grandpa Bebe fire up a small green tractor before she returned to the shelter. It was playtime! With the cats, she crawled through the play structure, giggling as they batted tiny paws at her from around corners, anticipating her approach. Next, she walked each dog up and down the roads, then threw toys for them to chase in one of the fenced meadows before returning them, panting and happy, to their kennels.

"Your turn, Scout," Tia said, ruffling the top of his head. "I haven't forgotten you!" She threw a tennis ball and laughed as the big dog bounded back with a damp and muddy stick he'd wrestled from a tangle of last year's tall yellow grass. "Guess you're not a retriever."

A little more play and then it was time for the afternoon feeding. At first, the little Chihuahua wouldn't touch his food, but after Tia sat with him for a minute and gave him an extra cuddle, he licked her on the chin, trotted over to his bowl, and began eating.

Satisfied that every canine and feline appetite was satiated, she rubbed bellies and scritched behind ears, then gave each animal a treat before returning to the office.

"*Qwawk!*"

Tia grinned at the raven sitting on top of his cage. "Don't worry, Raphael, I saved one for you." Raphael hopped over, tilted his head sideways at her, and accepted the offered biscuit.

So far, Tia had spent her entire first day with the cats and dogs—and Raphael, though he pretty much looked after himself—but Grandpa Bebe had told her to find him in the barn after she'd finished the afternoon feeding. She hoped that meant that she would get to work with the horses. She loved the way they looked, the way they moved, and even the way they smelled.

After blowing a kiss at Raphael, who bobbed his head as if to catch it, Tia made her way to the barn. There were two doors, the first acting as a buffer to the outside, which was probably a good thing considering how cold the winter wind could blow. With her hand on the door handle, she felt the unmistakable sensation of someone watching her. She spun around and laughed.

"Hi Horatio!"

The goat bleated and scooted back around the corner. "You're definitely a shy boy," she called after him.

Horatio reminded her of a story she'd heard at her old school. It was early last September. A class visitor had read from a book about a boy who had been found living in the mountains with a herd of goats. No one knew how long the boy had been there, but he ran around on all fours and would bleat like a goat instead of speaking.

Tia couldn't wait to get home and tell Mama. She and Tag had taken the bus home, like always, and run all the way up the stairs to their apartment. But Mama hadn't been home.

They'd waited, had cheese-and-cracker sandwiches for supper, then went to look for her. They went to the grocery store, a park Mama liked, the café where she worked, even the school, and finally found her sitting with friends on the patio of a restaurant not far from home. She'd laughed and pinched Tia's cheek, which was embarrassing, and said, "It's about time you found me!" Like it was all some big game.

Tia sighed and entered the barn.

Inside, she saw a horse peeking at her from a stall. The nameplate fastened to the boards said *Brenna*. She was a light chestnut colour with a white mane and tail. Ears perked toward her, the horse whickered.

Following the sounds of a radio, which Tia figured must be Grandpa Bebe's office, she made her way slowly down the aisle, reading the nameplates and saying hello to each horse as she passed.

Many horses were outside in the paddocks, but not all. Grandpa Bebe had told her that people from the area leased some of the horses, and if he knew they were coming by, he'd leave their horses in stalls for them.

It must be wonderful to be able to ride a horse whenever you wanted. Not that she even knew how. Maybe, if she worked hard, Grandpa Bebe would teach her.

No. She couldn't think like that. Yesterday's incident with the rock had been a reminder of how quickly something might happen and get them booted out of one home into the next. It would only stop when she found Mama, and Tia and Tag were back where they belonged.

Stay focussed, Tia. She's out there somewhere. She needs you.

Beside the box stalls, there were several empty standing stalls. Those did not have gates, but were open to the aisle. Horses walked in and stood as if they were in a car-park. Right before Grandpa Bebe's office, there were three more box stalls, the last one extra wide, which was good, because there was an extra-wide horse inside it.

"Hello, girl," Tia said to Disa, keeping her voice soft.

"She likes you."

Tia turned around and saw Grandpa Bebe standing in the doorway to the office. "Why is she in such a big stall?"

"She's pregnant. This is our foaling stall."

Of course. That was why she was so large.

"How did she get pregnant?" Tia asked, then blushed. "I mean, I know how it works, but I didn't see a stallion."

Grandpa Bebe smiled. "I drove her all the way to South Dakota. There's a stallion down there that throws nice foals. I've used him before."

"Will she have her baby soon?" Tia asked.

Grandpa Bebe shook his head. "I hope not. She's not due for a few more weeks, but she was bleeding a little, so I'm keeping her inside in the hopes that she'll stay calm—and not take off with the rest of that lot again."

"Do they get loose often?"

"Garri is a genius escape artist. I think I've got the latch fixed pretty good this time. If he figures it out again, I'll have to take him on the road, join a circus act or something."

Tia grinned. "Won't she get lonely for the others?"

Grandpa Bebe motioned toward the stall next to Disa's. "That's why Dinni is inside too."

As if she knew they were talking about her, Dinni whickered from the adjoining stall.

Disa closed her eyes a little as Grandpa Bebe stroked her

nose. Her bottom lip fluttered and then hung as if she were totally relaxed and content.

"What happens when it's time for the baby to come out? Do you have to take her to the vet?"

"No, she's fine right here. Most of the time horses don't even need our help."

"She sure is big," Tia said. "How many babies do horses usually have at one time?"

"Usually just one but twins can happen. As a matter of fact, Disa had twins the last time we bred her, but there's just one this time."

"Are her other babies here?"

Grandpa Bebe considered for a moment, as if deciding whether or not to answer. "Just one," he said. "Dinni was one of her twins, but the other one didn't make it."

"Oh." Tia swallowed hard, feeling a sudden pang for an animal she never knew.

"It's nature's way. When they're growing in Mama's belly, one foal usually gets more nourishment and is born stronger. Dinni's brother died before he was born."

Tia stroked Disa's neck, wondering if she missed her babies or even knew that one hadn't made it. "Everything will be okay this time, though. Right?"

"I'm sure everything will be perfect," Grandpa Bebe said, his voice rich and rumbly. "The vet checked her out when she was bleeding and said that apart from that, she's coming along just fine."

"Will the bleeding stop?"

"Already has."

From the corner of her eye, Tia saw commotion. "Scout!" she cried. He'd pushed open the door from the office and was walking toward her, wagging his whole body as if he hadn't just seen her a few hours ago.

"Hello, Scout!" Grandpa Bebe called out. "I see you've finished your nap."

Tia thought about how easily Grandpa Bebe had accepted him, as if it were no big deal. "Thanks for letting him stay with you," she said, petting him.

"He's good company. The horses like him too."

"When he's not barking at them, you mean."

Grandpa Bebe patted his leg, and Scout waggled over. "Actually, he's been quiet, which is good. I was worried that he would chase them and make a lot of noise. If he does that, he might get kicked."

"He barked plenty when we first ran into them out on the road."

"Maybe he knows they're back where they belong, so he's taking it easy." He ruffled Scout behind the ears. "Isn't that right, Scout?"

In answer, Scout sat, thumping his tail and leaning against Grandpa Bebe's leg.

There was something worrying her. Something she had to say. "Hey, Grandpa Bebe?"

He raised his eyebrows in a question.

"You know that stuff Tag said about going to Winnipeg?"

"I remember."

"He was just mixed up. You don't have to tell Cathy and Bob about it."

"I figured it was just a mistake. Is that what it was? A mistake?" His voice was soft, his eyes serious.

"Yeah."

"Then I guess there is nothing to mention."

"Okay. Thanks. For that, and for ... well, everything. It was fun today. Do you have anything else for me to do?"

"Hmm." Grandpa Bebe narrowed his eyes, then nodded and gave Scout one more pat. "If you're all finished at the shelter, would you like to learn how to groom?"

Tia's stomach leaped. "Yes! Oh, yes, please! I'd like that a lot."

Grandpa Bebe grabbed what looked like the same, knotty rope halter he'd had the other day and motioned for Tia to follow him outside. "Garri here loves a good brushing," he said once they'd reached the paddock. "Watch how I put his halter on. Over the nose, then behind the ears. Want to try?"

She nodded, amazed at how quietly Garri stood while Grandpa Bebe took the halter off for her to give it a go. It took a couple of tries, but with Grandpa Bebe there to guide her, Tia soon got it right.

Next, Grandpa Bebe attached a lead rope to the halter. He walked Garri in a circle, explaining what to do if he, or another horse, didn't walk nicely beside her. "Remember that you're the boss. You lead, not the other way around." He handed her the rope.

Tia wasn't sure what walking had to do with grooming but she didn't ask. She was over the moon to be walking beside this magnificent animal. Not just walking, but leading! When she stopped, Garri did too. Same when she took a step forward.

Grandpa Bebe opened the barn door and motioned for her to take Garri inside to the grooming area. Scout wagged his tail in encouragement.

There were horse-high rings in the wall, each spaced a few feet apart. Grandpa Bebe showed her how to fasten the lead rope to it, then made her tie and untie it until she was comfortable. "I'll give you a halter and lead to take home with you," he said. "Practise until you can do it with your eyes closed."

Then came the brushing. First the currycomb, round and round on Garri's neck, back and belly, then a scrubby mitt made of soft, rubber bristles on his legs and nose. Next came the hard bush, followed by the soft brush, and finally a comb for his mane and tail. In the end, the dirt that had been hidden in Garri's coat was transferred quite thoroughly onto Tia.

"You have enough strength for another?" Grandpa Bebe asked.

Tia nodded. Her arms were tired, but she didn't want to stop. Not yet.

"Okay, let's see you take Garri back to the paddock, and you can give Dinni a brush.

Dinni was hardly dirty at all on account of spending most of the day inside. As Tia finished, she looked over the stall wall at Disa, who was gazing back at her. There was something about her eyes. She felt a pang of longing as recognition dawned. Big, soft, and kind. They reminded her of Mama.

"Can I brush Disa too, Grandpa Bebe?" Tia asked.

He smiled. "I don't see why not." He reached over Disa's stall door and scratched her under her chin. "She does get cranky sometimes being cooped up like this, but she seems content enough right now. Make sure to tie her up, even in her stall, and watch her ears in case she has any sore spots. If she flicks them backward, back off a little. That's her way of letting you know."

Happily, Tia got to work. So completely absorbed she was in her task, she jumped when Grandpa Bebe spoke a short time later. "You're doing a fine job, Tia. Can I leave you alone?"

"Of course!"

"Right then. I'll be in the back paddock if you need me."

Disa loved the attention. When Tia reached an itchy spot with the currycomb, the horse moaned and leaned into her, eyes halfway closed. "Lovely mama," Tia cooed. "So patient. So good. I'm going to make you shine."

Finished at last, Tia placed the brushes outside the stall, giving faithful Scout a pat on the head, then returned to release Disa from her lead and halter. Instead of moving away, the horse placed her head on Tia's shoulder and sighed.

Suddenly choked with awe and something else, something big she couldn't name, Tia returned the hug. And then she knew.

She was in love.

Chapter Six

She was in a house she both knew and didn't know. It was their apartment in Winnipeg, but also different, as it had many more than their two bedrooms. She was hurrying to make beds that weren't supposed to be there, but every time she made one, it would suddenly be unmade. Except for Mama's. That bed stayed perfect.

She jogged down the long, yellow hall, past the picture of a fish that Tag had scribbled on with marker and they hadn't quite scrubbed away, and finally reached the kitchen. Mama was sitting at the chipped tile table in the kitchen where they had breakfast every morning. Her head was tilted down, and she was looking at a photo album.

"Let me see, Mama, let me see," Tia said, over and over.

But no matter how many times she said it, Mama wouldn't look up and show her the photos. Why wouldn't she look at her?

Tia awoke in a sweat, her heart pounding so hard, it was a wonder it hadn't woken the house. She felt ill and something else.

Guilty?

She cleared her throat and pushed herself up on her elbows. Dreams were weird like that. They made no sense.

But why wouldn't Mama look at her?

Through the gingham curtains on her window, which she kept open so she could see the sky, Tia saw vivid swaths of violet, fuchsia and mandarin pushing away the remnants of night. She padded across the floor, stood at the window and watched until a raven arced across the lake toward the woods. It pulled her attention back down to the earth, toward Ice Pony Ranch, where just yesterday she'd found the best and most lovely animal friend of them all: Disa.

Grandpa Bebe and Jennifer were probably already awake and feeding the animals. Mornings and late afternoons were the busiest times at the ranch and shelter. They could probably use a hand.

Tia briefly remembered Cathy and her rules. "Not every day," she'd said. "Every two days at most."

After figuring out when Tia was likely to have the most homework and taking into account family game night, Tia and Cathy had agreed that she would work Tuesdays and Fridays after supper and then Sunday all day.

But they hadn't talked about early mornings.

Tia thought about it for a moment. She would be back home well before the school bus arrived to carry her and Tag off to town. She wouldn't miss a thing.

With electricity sparking through her veins, she pulled on blue jeans and a cable-knit sweater. She brushed her teeth, scribbled a quick note, which she left on the kitchen table, and then hurried out the door.

She felt a surge of excitement. *If I get there quick enough, maybe I can give Disa her breakfast grain!*

Tia reached the barn and Horatio scooted away, bleating. "It's okay, little guy. We're going to be friends, I promise. You won't be shy forever."

Through the doors, she heard commotion. Inside, she was met by a glorious cacophony of whinnying, stomping and trotting, as horses, released from their stalls, made their way to the outdoor paddocks.

"Stay back!" came a bellow over the chaos. It was Grandpa Bebe. "Out!"

After a second of stunned paralysis, Tia ducked back between the doors and left the barn. She was confused, her head suddenly pounding, and she blinked hard to keep hurt from spilling out in tears. What was that all about? Grandpa Bebe had been so kind to her, made her feel appreciated and needed. Why didn't he want her there now?

It's not fair, Tia thought. *I was only trying to do something helpful.*

She was almost to the road when Grandpa Bebe's voice stopped her again.

"Hang on, Tia, come back here." There was no trace of the outrage she'd heard in the barn.

"Forget it!" she shouted. A person's true colours always show when they don't have time to paint on something else. What was he going to say? That he was just kidding? That he was as nice as he'd obviously just pretended to be when she and Tag had first stumbled across him and his horses?

She could hear him catching up. "Hang on, Tia. Please," he puffed. He put a hand on her shoulder, forcing her to stop.

He looked hard at her, his bushy eyebrows smashed together in the middle. "You can't do that!"

Tia felt her mouth drop open in surprise. She'd expected an apology—or an excuse. Not this. "I ... do what?"

Grandpa Bebe put his hand to his forehead and rubbed it. "Did we not talk about feeding-time safety?"

Tia shook her head, still on the verge of tears but repelling the emotion that threatened to pummel her into someone smaller than she wanted to be. She would not, must not, show weakness. Grandpa Bebe had yelled at her for no reason. *He* was the one who should be upset, not her.

Grandpa Bebe took a deep breath. "Okay, that's on me. I'm sorry I yelled. Come on up to the barn. We'll have some hot cocoa and go over a few ground rules. Okay?"

Huh?

Tia hesitated, then followed. She hadn't actually expected him to apologize, just like that. Part of her felt like staying mad, but the thought of hot cocoa was inviting. She'd left the house without putting anything in her belly.

When they reached the barn office, they found a plate with four buns waiting beside a dish of butter and a knife. The buns were in rectangle shapes twisted in the middle so that they looked like pastry bow ties. They were still steaming, smelled warm, buttery, heavenly.

"Ostaslaufur!" Grandpa Bebe cried out.

"Um, gesundheit?" Tia teased.

"Jennifer's been baking this morning. These are Icelandic cheese buns. My favourite."

Icelandic horses, Icelandic buns ... "Are you Icelandic?"

"My last name is Arnason. My great-great-grandfather arrived here from Iceland a little over 100 years ago, back when this area was still known as New Iceland."

"Was he an explorer or something?"

Grandpa Bebe chuckled. "Not quite. Icelanders first came here in 1875, after volcanic eruptions in Iceland made life very difficult. They thought this might be their new homeland. Gimli was the first town. It means 'paradise' in Icelandic."

"But there is still an Iceland."

"There is! People are made of tough stuff. They survive. Speaking of surviving, let's go over those barn rules!"

"Okay."

Eyeing the cheese buns, she sat and took in her surroundings while Grandpa Bebe plugged in the kettle to make cocoa.

Calling it an office was a stretch. There was no filing cabinet or computer like in the shelter office, and Grandpa Bebe's desk was little more than a small kitchen table with two chairs. It was more like a resting space with shelves holding mysterious jars and squeeze-tubes. Horse medicines, maybe.

Grandpa Bebe set two mugs of steaming cocoa on the desk and sat down. "First off, you call out 'Door!' before opening one." He paused. "Are you listening, Tia? It's really important."

"Uh-huh," she answered, and she was, but gosh those cheese buns looked good.

"Go ahead," Grandpa Bebe said, smiling.

"Thanks!"

She took one that had cheese filling squishing through a centre twist. The bun was perfectly warm and moist, which meant her fingers sunk into the sides of it just a bit, but didn't moosh through.

"Remember," Grandpa Bebe said, "unless you have x-ray vision, you never know if there's going to be a horse on the other side. They startle easily, and any person next to a horse or riding one might get stepped on or thrown if it bolts."

Grandpa Bebe continued with rules as she broke the bun in half, inhaling the sweet scent.

"And when horses are running in and out, you can't be anywhere near where you might get stepped on. Like this morning!"

"I get it," she said.

"You sure?"

She tried to look solemn to show that she understood the seriousness of the situation, but her anticipation of the pastry twists made her mouth water and her soul dance. She broke into a broad smile. "I do now. Promise." She spread the middle of her pastry with butter and bit in, letting the butter drip down her chin before catching it with a paper napkin.

"Good! And I already told you about leaving gates and doors as you find them."

Tia spread more butter on for another bite. She'd never tasted anything better. Bite, chew, swallow. Yum.

"So, are we clear?" Grandpa Bebe asked.

Tia nodded, wiping a last smear of butter from her chin, the bun entirely gone, even the crumbs. "I just thought you might need some help. You know, with feeding."

"That's good of you, Tia. Feeding time is busy, but I've got an even bigger job if you have time."

"Sure!"

Grandpa Bebe frowned. "Hang on. Don't you have school?"

"Later." In her hurry to leave the house, she'd forgotten her watch, but that had been only, like, fifteen minutes ago. She'd left the house even before Cathy had come down to make breakfast, which was usually crazy early. She'd keep an eye on the clock in the barn. It would be fine.

Grandpa Bebe's eyes twinkled. "You might not be so excited when I show you what it is."

In a blink, Tia had a pitchfork in hand and was cleaning out stalls. If Grandpa Bebe thought she wouldn't like this, boy was he wrong. Sure, it was poo, but it wasn't as gross as the poo from some of the other animals Tia had cleaned up after. It didn't even smell that bad. She supposed it was because of what horses ate: grain, alfalfa and sweet hay.

Tia set aside her poo musings and focussed on the rhythm of the fork. As she worked, she revelled in the ache in her arms and back. It felt real. Honest. It was easy to lose herself in the sounds of the pitchfork scraping boards, Grandpa Bebe sweeping, and Disa snoring two stalls down.

Dinni was out for her morning exercise, so when Tia got to Disa's stall, she moved her temporarily to Dinni's space. Afterward, back in her usual stall, Disa rested her chin on Tia's shoulder and sighed, just as she had the day before. This time, as Tia hugged her, she rubbed behind Disa's ear and was rewarded with a contented groan.

Best. Horse. Ever.

Tia wondered what kind of a mother Disa would be. Probably pretty good. After all, Dinni turned out fine. From what she'd seen on TV and driving along highways beside fields, horses mostly just let their babies run around wherever they wanted. They knew they would come back when they were hungry, or maybe if they were hurt and needed comfort.

Mama was kind of like that, too.

Tia remembered once, when she was younger, she'd gotten mad because Mama wouldn't take her to the water park where some kid on the street was supposed to be having their birthday party. She'd decided to make Mama unhappy, just like she was unhappy, by making her think she'd run away. Tia hid in her closet for hours. She'd waited and waited for Mama to call out, all worried and looking for her, but the call had never come. Eventually, she'd fallen asleep.

The next morning, Tia had found Mama sound asleep in her own bed and had asked why she hadn't come looking for her. Mama had looked confused at first as she rubbed her head and slapped her bedside table looking for the bottle of pills she always kept there. She said she'd figured Tia just needed some time to herself.

Like a horse, Mama let her be free. She wasn't smothering, like some mothers. Like Cathy. Cathy had to know where Summer and Daye were and what they were doing every minute of every day. Especially since the rock incident.

She felt a small stab of guilt.

As if on cue, the barn door swung open, and there she stood. Fake mom.

"Were you planning on going to school today, Tia?" Cathy asked. She had one hand on hip, brows furrowed.

Oh! Tia glanced up at the barn clock. 8:45! She'd missed the bus. School would start in fifteen minutes.

Grandpa Bebe looked at her, his brows smashed together like he was trying to figure something out.

"Sorry, Cathy," Grandpa Bebe said. "I just figured …" He looked again at Tia. "A misunderstanding, I think."

Cathy shook her head. "Don't give it a second thought, Grandpa Bebe." Although Cathy didn't speak the words out loud, her stern look clearly meant: *She's not even supposed to be here today.*

Tia winced when she saw Grandpa Bebe looking at her in much the same way. Wishing she could disappear through a trap door, she pushed the straw in Disa's stall around with her foot. Not that she actually thought there would be a trap door, but … well, you never knew.

"Come on, then," Cathy said.

Cathy didn't say two words as she drove Tia to school, which meant she was *really* mad. Otherwise she would have insisted Tia stop at the house to change. She was definitely sporting *Eau de Pony*.

"We'll talk about this later," Cathy said, pulling up in front of the school.

Tia knew what that really meant—that she needed to fine-tune her punishment. She felt a brief twinge of panic that Cathy might send her and Tag away, boot them toward another placement.

Or … what if she changed her mind about letting Tia work at Ice Pony Ranch? If she did that, what did it even matter where they lived?

This was all so unfair!

Instead of thanking Cathy for the ride or apologizing, Tia slammed the door of the minivan and stomped into the school, making it inside just as the last bell rang, signalling she was late.

Tia closed her eyes. One more thing she'd be in trouble for. First Grandpa Bebe, then Cathy, and now this. How had this day that had begun gloriously so suddenly turned into a murky mess? She'd been an idiot to think she could have something good here. It was obvious there was only one place she truly fit, and that was with her mother. Her real one.

Like she'd suddenly had a bucket of ice water splooshed into her face, understanding dawned.

That was what the dream had meant, why Mama wouldn't look at her. When Mama needed her most, Tia had betrayed her by relaxing into this new life. It was up to Tia to find Mama, because no one else would.

There was something else bothering her. Something she hadn't told anyone, not even Tag. It was about what happened the night before Mama disappeared.

They'd had a fight. Sort of.

Tia was used to seeing Mama drink. Lots of times she'd have a bottle of wine on the go as she made supper or sometimes when she was home in the afternoon and just sitting and reading a book. Mostly she went out to drink and would come home after and go straight to bed—except for when she'd call home to say she'd be gone for the night, maybe a few nights. That had happened even more after she'd met Richard.

But then Tia had started finding empty bottles by the sink when she woke up in the morning. One, sometimes two. And there'd been more under the sink. Tia wasn't stupid. She'd seen commercials about people who had problems, they'd even talked about it at school. There was help for that.

That night before Mama disappeared, Tia saw that she was worried about something and asked her to say what it was. After all, Mama had raised Tia to be strong and smart. She thought maybe she could help.

But Mama had refused to tell her anything. Tia had gotten mad. She even yelled. That's when things went all wrong.

Tia had told Mama to get help. She told her about Alcoholics Anonymous.

Mama had looked at her then, something really strange in her eyes. Something Tia hadn't seen before. Something more than sad.

It had scared her.

"Go to bed, Tia," Mama had said, her voice barely more than a whisper. "Everything will be fine."

The next day, she was gone.

She hadn't abandoned them. Tia refused to believe that. She wouldn't. Not even if Tia had made her mad.

It couldn't be that. It just couldn't.

Mama needed Tia to help her. To find her. Tia owed her that, especially after making her more than sad.

Why hadn't she stayed up that night and made Mama talk some more? There was a tiny ember deep inside her belly that wanted to shoot up and make her believe this was all her fault. But she wouldn't let it. She was old enough to know that wasn't true. But still, the ember smouldered. Only one thing would make it go out. She had to fix this. She had to find Mama.

That meant she had to calm down and bide her time. The last time she'd tried to leave, she'd had no real plan. That's why it hadn't worked.

She watched through the office door as the school secretary typed at her computer keyboard.

Maybe she had a better plan. The start of one, anyhow.

She had access to the Internet and to a phone. She would find Richard that way. *First Richard, then Mama.*

Chapter Seven

Wind rustled budding branches as the departing school bus belched its way down the lane and Tia and Tag made their way toward the house. Tag had refused to sit beside Tia on the bus and now walked quickly, as if to put distance between them.

"Come on, Tag," Tia pleaded, trotting to catch up. "Don't be mad."

"You weren't there. I had to go by myself."

Tag hated taking the bus by himself. Tia knew that, and that made her mistake that morning even worse. She didn't care so much about letting down Cathy, but her brother had been through enough. "I know," she said. "Haven't you made any friends yet?"

"Not on the bus." He didn't slow, but at least he was talking to her. "Mom would have yelled at you."

"Maybe not. She loved animals too. She would have understood."

"She got really mad when I stayed after school that time."

"That's because she was worried about you." She felt a pang. She should have waited for him.

"She wasn't really worried about me. She doesn't even care about us."

Tia nearly stumbled. "How can you say that?"

"Because she left us. Because she's not coming back."

Tia felt like icy water had just been thrown over her. She grabbed hold of Tag and stopped him. "Don't say that. Don't ever say that."

Tag just looked at her, worry in his eyes. She drew him in and hugged him. "I know you didn't mean it, Tag. This is my fault." *Everything was her fault.* Nothing had been right since that last night with Mama. She let go and looked at him again. "You're right. I should have been on the bus with you. I'm sorry."

"Okay," he said, and shrugged.

They continued up the drive, this time side by side. On the porch, outside the door, Tia paused for a steadying breath.

"Aren't you going to open it?" Tag asked.

"Yeah, sure," Tia said, turning the handle. Her hand touched the folded note in her jacket pocket. Being late for class meant an automatic note home, which had to be signed by a parent or guardian.

Wistfully, she looked toward the garage where Bob liked to tinker with boat engines or craft rustic benches and chairs, and she wished he were there. Last night, he'd mentioned that he had to make an afternoon airport run to drop off departing guests and pick up new ones. That meant he might not be back until late. Too bad. He was way more easygoing than Cathy.

Tia toyed with the idea of "forgetting" about the note and catching Bob later, but she doubted that would work. He'd probably just give it to Cathy anyway. She was particular about being involved in anything school related. Actually, she was particular about knowing everything about everyone, especially stuff about Tia and Tag. Privacy didn't exist in Cathy's house.

But she couldn't know what was in Tia's head.

Tia followed her brother into the house.

Cathy was sitting at the kitchen table, the twins perched next to her on booster seats. Both girls had carrot sticks and creamy dip on plates in front of them. There were two other places set, each with a glass of milk and additional carrot sticks and dip. Tag slipped into a seat and reached for the milk.

"Have a seat, Tia," Cathy said. "I didn't have quite as many carrots as I thought. Enough to make a snack, though."

Tia gulped as Cathy looked at her. The carrots she'd taken for the horses would be one more strike against her. The dark pit she had to climb out of was growing deeper by the second.

Cathy peered at her. "Is something wrong? You look like you have something you want to say."

Maybe Cathy *could* read her mind.

"Yes," she said, "but it can wait until you have more time."

"I have time," Cathy said. "Come. Sit."

Tia ignored the place Cathy had set for her and pulled up a chair on the other side of Daye. "No thank you, Daye," she said softly to an offered bite of carrot.

Tag finished eating, and with a "Thanks for the snack!" he dashed down the hall toward his room.

Cathy smiled, watching him go, then turned back to Tia. Waiting.

"Um … a couple of things." Tia swallowed hard. "First, I am really, really sorry about this morning." She took a deep breath, then blurted out, "I thought Grandpa Bebe might need help with the feeding, but then I got it wrong and he was mad and gave me cocoa and let me clean the stalls." She swallowed hard. "I only meant to be a minute."

Cathy nodded. "Thank you for that, Tia. Grandpa Bebe did call while you were at school, but I'm glad you told me in your own words. It is important we are open with each other." She offered a glimmer of a smile. "Besides, I do understand the draw of the horses."

"You do?"

"You may find this hard to believe, but there was a time I was very much like you." Cathy paused, maybe noticing Tia's perplexed look. "No, I wasn't in foster care. I mean that like you, I loved every kind of animal, especially horses. My grandmother used to keep them, you know."

"She did?" Cathy had never mentioned her grandmother to Tia, or even her mother. There was still a whole lot Tia didn't know about this family.

Cathy's eyes glazed as though she was looking right back into her memory. "My grandmother adored horses and I adored her. Maybe that's the reason I wanted to do everything she did. Or maybe it was because we were so much alike." She shrugged. "Doesn't much matter. Worked out the same."

Cathy wiped Summer's hands and face with a wet cloth, then Daye's, and released them from their chairs. The twins sprinted off in the same direction, as if by unspoken plan.

"Every morning, she would feed her horses—she had three—and then clean the stalls. Like you, I figured she could use some help, so even before breakfast, I'd ride my bike over and give her a hand. Then after school, we'd saddle up and go for a ride."

"So you really do get it?" Tia asked.

Cathy nodded, smiling all the way to her eyes as she cleared away the remains of the snacks and wiped down the table. "My grandmother lived near a lake, and there was a little island not far from the shore. She'd swim her horse over and call for me to join her." She leaned against the kitchen sink, bunching the wiping cloth in her hands. "I could never get my horse to go. The water spooked him too much. Instead, I'd tie him up and swim." She looked wistful. "It was a nice time, but I always wished my horse would get in the water and carry me over, just like my grandmother's horse did with her."

"Did you keep trying?" Tia asked, engrossed in the story. "You should never give up on something that's important to you."

"I agree with you, Tia, and I did try for a while. But then my grandmother died, and horses just didn't seem important anymore."

Tia felt a wash of disappointment. Cathy didn't get it after all. Not completely. Tia would never stop loving animals, not for any reason, even if someone died.

Just like she would never give up on her mother.

But she wouldn't say that to Cathy. Not when she was so obviously still hurting from her memories. Instead, she said, "I'm sorry your grandmother died."

"Me too," Cathy said with a sad smile. "But that was a long time ago. I just want you to know that I do understand the appeal, however, we still have to have ground rules."

Tia nodded. "Grandpa Bebe said the same thing."

"This is a busy household, Tia. Without ground rules, we won't know who's coming and going and when. We also need to make sure you're safe. Grandpa Bebe told me how you walked in when the horses were racing for the door." Cathy swallowed hard, then shook her head. "I can't tell you how much it scares me to think of you getting hurt."

That was unexpected. Tia didn't know what to say.

"Tell you what," Cathy said. "No weekday mornings at the shelter. Not yet." She looked like she thought Tia might argue. "Let's stick to what we've already agreed to. If you keep up with your homework, and there are no other unexpected hiccups, we'll talk about more. Can you live with that?"

"What about school holidays?"

She reached for Tia's hand as if she might grab hold, stopped, and gave it a quick pat instead. "I'd like us to do family things on holidays, okay? After a month or so, we can talk about this again."

Tia's heart swelled with gratitude. This so easily could have gone the other way. "Okay."

Cathy tipped her head to the side and studied her. "Are you absolutely certain, Tia? I can't have you saying you agree to something and then going back on it. And no bending the rules. Only agree if you mean it."

"I agree, really, I do!" Tia assured her. "I won't mess up again. I promise."

Cathy smiled. "I appreciate that, Tia." She stood. "I thought I might dash to the grocery store before supper," she said. "If you don't mind watching the twins, that is."

"No ... I mean, yes." Tia cleared her throat. "I don't mind. Sure."

Wow. So not what she expected. Cathy was trusting her with the twins. She'd anticipated punishment, not this.

Cathy plucked her jacket from a hook by the door and turned. "Sorry, was there something else? You said there were a couple of things."

The note! It suddenly felt warm in her pocket. Tia took a breath, pinched the sharp, folded corner of it between her fingers, and pulled it out.

"What's that?" Cathy asked.

"I was late for school," she said, her voice barely louder than a whisper.

Cathy looked tired as she took the note from her. "It's fine, Tia. I won't be long."

Chapter Eight

After dinner, Tia finished her homework and flopped onto her bed. What a crazy, stupid day. It was crazy nice that Cathy finally trusted her to watch the twins, especially when Cathy could just as easily have washed her hands of her. Grandpa Bebe might have done the same, the way she'd stormed into the barn that way. She understood now that he had only been angry because she might have gotten hurt. She'd heard the horses running by before she even opened the door. Why hadn't she waited?

Why, why, why do I always mess up? That was the stupid part.

She never used to. Not like this. Nothing had been right since the day they'd been taken from their home.

On her bedside table, she spotted the decoupage box that she'd carried with her to every placement. She picked it up and pried off the lid. Inside, she kept a few small treasures, worth nothing to others, but everything to her. It made her feel better sometimes to hold each item and remember.

There was a key to the apartment she hoped one day they would return to, even though their social worker had said it had been rented out to someone else.

Next to the key, there was a dime-sized pressed flower, a once-brilliant blue blossom with a cheery, yellow centre. She and Mama had found growing it through a crack in the sidewalk outside their apartment building. Tia smiled, remembering how her mother had called it a "pinch flower," not knowing the real name. Tia had looked it up later and saw it was called a forget-me-not.

Lining the bottom of the box, there were three folded strips of photos from a coin-operated booth they'd visited in a mall. She pulled them out and looked at them, running her finger along their edges, thinking how fun that day had been. One strip had photos of Tia and Tag making funny faces and poses. The second: Tia, Tag and Mama. It was too hard to look at that one. She folded it up and put it back in the box. The third showed Mama and a man. He had long hair, tattoos and a nice smile: Richard.

She returned her treasures to the box, picked up one of her school notebooks and made her way to the computer in the hall. If anyone asked what she was doing, she'd just say she was doing research for a school project.

With a quick glance over her shoulder, Tia logged on to the Internet and opened a search-engine page. She typed in *Hotels, Winnipeg.*

Almost immediately, the screen was flooded with results. More than twenty-five million hotels? No way that could be right. There were only about 750,000 people living in and around the city. She knew because they'd talked about it in class.

Way too many. Need to narrow it down. Tia clicked on the *Maps* option.

Better. The little red dots in the map image of the city she could work with. There were still a lot of them, but it was way better than twenty-five million possibilities. Tia clicked on each dot and recorded the contact information that popped up.

Her stomach rumbled and she glanced at the clock on the corner of the computer screen. She'd been at this for forty-five minutes already! Luckily, she was almost finished.

Tia jumped as Cathy poked her head around the corner. "Tia, would you mind finding your brother? It'll be getting dark soon."

Tia quickly closed the map. "How come you don't know where he is?" she snarked, immediately kicking herself. Cathy had been pretty decent to her today. It was like Tia couldn't help snapping at her.

Cathy didn't call Tia on her attitude. Instead, she said, "I think he's in the yard" and disappeared back around the corner.

Tia returned her notebook to her schoolbag, then went out in the yard to look for Tag. Not there. Not at the beach, either, where he sometimes liked to skip stones. She made her way back up to the front of the house where Cathy had a garden plot. It was dormant now, but she'd been talking about how she couldn't wait to put in peas, corn and potatoes. When Tia had mentioned that she and Mama had planted sunflowers one summer right after Tag had been born, Cathy had offered to put in a few of those too.

What Tia hadn't mentioned was that Mama had forgotten about the flowers. They hadn't watered or weeded them and by the end of the summer, there were no happy, big-faced yellow flowers bowing under the weight of their seed. There was nothing at all except a tangle of stinkweed.

That was the summer Daddy had died. Everything had changed then. Mama had changed, and then nothing else was the same.

Bob had just pulled up to the house in the van and was unloading bags from the trunk. A man and a woman in matching green windbreakers, clearly the new guests, were standing close by.

"Hi," Tia called, waving. The lodge guests smiled and Tia turned to Bob. "Have you seen Tag?"

Bob nodded. "Top of the drive. He's riding that old bike he found in the shed. Said he wouldn't go far."

Tia nodded her thanks and jogged up the drive. Tag was riding figure-eights in the lane. "Tag!" she called. "Time to come in!"

Tag stopped riding, turning his head toward the field on the other side of the lane.

Tia frowned. Her brother didn't look his usual happy and slightly annoying self. "Something wrong?"

He turned back toward her as she drew close. "I like it here, Tia."

"I know. Why does that make you sad?"

"It doesn't. I'm just afraid you're going to wreck everything."

Tia felt like she'd been stabbed. "I'm not wrecking anything, Tag."

Tag looked like he was going to cry. "I miss Mama," he said, his voice husky. "But it's nice here." He turned the bike around and, with wheels spitting gravel, took off up the lane.

"Tag, wait!" Tia called, running after him. Just outside the cemetery, she finally caught up, but only because he'd skidded to a stop. He climbed off the bike, dropped it and stood still, tears running down his cheeks. "Hey," she said, reaching for him. "It's okay, Tag."

"No," he said, pushing her away. Tia stood, arms at her side, until finally his tears stopped and he sat on the ground. He had his back to the cemetery but kept glancing over his shoulder at it.

Tia sat beside him. "Want to tell me what's going on?"

Tag took a deep breath and snuck one more look at the cemetery. "Do you remember that time Mama helped with the Halloween party?"

She nodded. It had been back when Tag was in kindergarten. Mama had been working at the corner store and her boss had been really good about letting her have time off when she asked for it. Tia remembered feeling jealous because Mama had never helped with any of her school parties.

"Mama said I needed to tell ghost stories," Tag told her, his voice really small.

"I don't remember that."

"She took me to the graveyard. She said that was the best place to learn ghost stories."

Tia felt the hair on the back of her neck prickle. Why didn't she remember this?

"She was acting funny."

Tia knew what that meant. It was the code she and Tag always used for when Mama had been drinking.

"She said she would be right back."

Tag started crying again, but when Tia reached for him, again, he pushed her away. She waited, but he just sat there, pushing stones around in the dirt. Finally, she asked, "Did she come back?"

"She left me there." He sounded angry. "She left me there until really late and I was really cold and I heard things that were really creepy, but I couldn't leave because she said she would come back. I didn't want her to think I was lost." He stood and started walking back toward the lodge.

She grabbed hold of his arm, stopping him. "Tag—"

He looked tired. "Tia, I love Mama, I do, and I feel so bad because I like it here." He started crying again. "I'm sorry."

Tia's head was spinning. She wanted to tell Tag that he wasn't remembering things right, but she couldn't. She knew what Mama could be like sometimes. And hearing Tag's story, she finally understood his fear of cemeteries. She couldn't really blame her brother for wanting a nice, ordinary place to stay, a place without loud parties or a mama who would suddenly get angry and yell for no reason. That had happened sometimes too.

"You don't have to be sorry, Tag," Tia said. With Mama gone, it was up to her to make sure everything was okay and that it would stay that way. "I'm not going to wreck things."

"Do you promise?" He held her eyes, unblinking.

Tia nodded. "Yes."

"Show me your hands and say it."

She showed him that she wasn't making the fib-cross with her fingers. "I promise. Now come on, let's get back."

After a long moment, Tag nodded, walking with her back to the main house. In the dining room, Bob and the twins were seated at one of the four large tables working on a wooden puzzle. Cathy was chatting and sipping tea at another table with the new guests.

"There they are!" Bob said, smiling as Tia and Tag entered. "Who's up for ginger cake before bed?"

After their snack, Tia cleared the dishes. She was halfway done before she realized she'd done it without even being ordered. Not that Cathy ever ordered, exactly. Tia swooped her hands through soapy water, listening to the bustle as everyone pitched in, wiping the counter and putting things away. Well, everyone except the twins, who had been tucked into bed.

Once everyone was settled for the night, Tia slipped back into the computer nook to send emails.

Dear Madam or Sir, she wrote, remembering her letter-writing etiquette from school. *I am writing to inquire two things. 1) Who owns your hotel? 2) If the owner's name is Richard, can you please have him contact me?*

She cut and pasted the same note for each hotel with an email address. The phone calls would take longer, but at least she'd done something, which was infinitely better than nothing.

Tia pushed herself back from the computer, yawning.

On her way to her room, she spotted a homemade card on the oak bookcase. It was made of red construction paper and had little heart stickers all over the cover. Inside, there were three words drawn in spidery letters with green and blue crayon: *Mom, Daye,* and *Summer.*

Tia set the card back on the shelf, glancing at the photo albums lined up neatly behind. Curious, she pulled one out. It was the kind of album people dressed up with fabric on the cover and lace trim. From the teddy-bear pattern, Tia guessed that inside she would find baby pictures. She did.

Warmth spread through her. She smiled as she flipped through photos from Daye and Summer as newborns, faces red and puffy, to the twins propped in their onesies in corners of a big armchair, to them being strapped in duel-seat strollers. In nearly every photo, they sported huge, open-mouthed smiles as identical as their outfits. Tia wondered at what point Cathy had started dressing the girls differently from each other. Maybe it had been their choice. How old does a kid need to be to decide they don't agree with everything their mother does?

How old had Tia been?

Tia glanced over her shoulder, suddenly awash with a feeling that she had done something wrong. She hadn't. It wasn't like she'd snooped through drawers. The photo albums were in plain sight for anyone to look at.

With a sigh, Tia returned the album. Then she picked up the handmade card again and flipped it over. No birthday mentioned and Mother's Day wasn't until next month.

Tia swallowed a lump in her throat and set the card back in its place.

Chapter Nine

Though it wasn't easy, for two weeks Tia had stuck to her word and only went to the barn Tuesday and Friday evenings. But oh, Sunday! That was her favourite day, as she could spend the whole length of it at the shelter, which also meant more time with Disa.

But more time meant deeper attachment, and a whole lot more worry.

The thumping of her heart was almost painful as she watched Grandpa Bebe examine Disa. If only she'd checked on the mare sooner!

Finally, he turned away from the horse, moved the straw around in her stall and then looked up at Tia with a smile. "It's good that you told me she wasn't eating, Tia, but I think she's fine."

"So it's not colic?" Tia asked, still feeling fluttery as she leaned against the inside of the stall door. It had shocked her after lunch to find Disa's feeding bin untouched. She should have gobbled it up hours ago.

From a favourite horse forum, Tia had learned that colic was an illness that came from food bunching in a horse's guts, and that it could be deadly. A horse refusing its grain was one of the signs.

"She's still drinking plenty of water." Grandpa Bebe assured her "See? The straw is wet from her pee. Her heart rate and temperature are normal, and she doesn't look like she's in any pain."

"So why won't she eat?"

Grandpa Bebe shrugged. "Not unusual towards the end of a pregnancy, Tia. She's got a big, ol' baby in there. I expect she'll be hungry again once the baby shifts and she can feel the empty spot in her stomach."

Disa did look pretty content, especially now that Grandpa Bebe had stopped poking around her belly. Her eyes were half closed and her bottom lip hung down as if she was too tired to hold up the weight of it.

"I guess that makes sense."

Grandpa Bebe stretched, yawned and rubbed his eyes. "Well, I guess I should file some notes."

Tia smiled. "Is that code for a nap?"

He laughed. "Smarty-pants!"

As Grandpa Bebe closed his office door behind him, Tia looked out the barn window toward the house. She could see Jennifer at the table, her head tilted down. She'd said she liked to do her paperwork there, rather than in the shelter office, because she could look out into the yard.

It was a short, cosmic gift of time and opportunity.

Setting her pitchfork down, she started formulating excuses, just in case:

I needed to call home about ... something.

I needed a tissue.

With Scout at her heels, Tia jogged from barn to shelter, greeted Raphael's hello squawk, ensured his cage door was open so he could stretch his wings and legs, then settled herself at the desk. She pulled two loose-leaf pages of hotel names and phone numbers from her pocket and smoothed them flat beside the telephone. These were the ones remaining after she'd exhausted all those with email addresses. They had to be called, old-style, which took so much more time. Frustrating! She was sure she'd have found Richard by now.

Carefully, she picked up the phone, put it to her ear, and listened.

The line was clear.

Tia pulled a pen from the desk drawer and put a mark beside the first of what looked like a few hundred Winnipeg hotels listed on the phonebook pages. Taking a deep breath, she dialed the number.

"Oh, hello," she said when someone answered. "I'm looking for a phone number for Richard ... no, not a guest, he owns it." As she spoke, doubt wiggled in. Had Richard been teasing her about owning a hotel? Two weeks of negative responses were wearing on her faith. "Or maybe he works there ... okay, I understand."

It didn't take long to learn that hotels wouldn't give out private information about employees, never mind owners. Maybe that was why hardly any had answered her emails.

After three calls, Tia had grown more confident with her approach. "Hello, I'd like the phone number for Richard who works at your hotel. I'm his niece, and there's been a family emergency."

Eight calls later, Tia had found one Richard, but he'd not been in. When the receptionist asked if Tia would like to leave a number, she refused and said she would call back later. If Richard called the barn when she wasn't there, there would be questions.

Tia glanced at the clock. She'd been calling hotels for twenty minutes and would now have finish her remaining chores in double-time.

She'd just finished tucking the cats and dogs in for the evening, when Jennifer opened the door to the shelter office and stuck her head inside. "Come on up to the house, Tia," she said. "I've been baking."

Tia's belly rumbled at the memory of Jennifer's Ostas-something cheese-buns. It was an invitation she couldn't resist. A few minutes later, settled at the kitchen table, she saw it wasn't buns that Jennifer had been baking, but a crazy-looking cake with more flat, thin layers than Tia could count.

"It's called a *Vinarterta*," Jennifer said.

"Is that Icelandic too? Icelandic horses, Icelandic cake, is everything in Iceland short?"

Jennifer laughed. "Even the trees. There is an old Icelandic saying that if you get lost in the woods in Iceland, you need only to stand up."

"Funny."

"But actually, no one is completely sure where the cake came from. Some say it came from Iceland with our first settlers, others say it was created here, and some people even say it came from somewhere else entirely."

"Foster cake."

"Pardon?"

Tia shrugged. "Just making a joke. Dumb, I guess."

"Oh, I ..." Jennifer looked embarrassed. "I guess moving around is pretty hard on you guys."

"It hasn't been great. I've never been any place like here, though. Thanks for giving me this job."

"We're glad to have you, Tia. You do good work."

She looked again at the cake. "I've never seen anyone bake stuff like you."

"My Grandma Gudny taught me her recipes before she passed, plus I worked for a long time at a bakery in town. I don't actually bake that much anymore. You've just caught me on a couple of lucky days. Want some milk with it?"

"Please!"

As Jennifer sliced the cake, she felt a glimmer of guilt for sneaking use of the phone. She knew that Jennifer and Grandpa Bebe probably wouldn't mind. But they might tell Cathy and Bob and then Tag might find out. She didn't want her brother to think she was jeopardizing anything, especially after promising him she wouldn't.

What would Mama think? Sure, she had her problems, but Mama had always insisted on honesty from her kids. The line between honest and dishonest was becoming fuzzy for Tia. Mama wouldn't like that. But she'd also taught Tia about putting family first.

Last summer, money had been particularly tight, so tight that Mama decided to sell the special locket Daddy had given her before he died. Luckily, Tia had a few dollars saved from babysitting and she insisted Mama use that instead. Mama had cried. She explained to Tia that she hadn't wanted to give up the necklace, but that it was her job to look after Tia and Tag. She said sometimes that meant doing things you never thought you would.

"Here's your foster cake," Jennifer teased, setting a slice in front of her along with a glass of milk.

Tia grinned. "You have to admit, it's easier to remember than that other name you said."

"*Vinarterta.*" Jennifer smiled. "You may be right."

As Jennifer sat, Tia noticed a necklace fall from between the folds of her shirt collar. "I like your necklace."

Jennifer touched her fingers to it, smiling softly. "Thanks. It was my grandmother's."

"My dad gave my mom a necklace kind of like that. I was just thinking about it."

"I bet it was special to her."

Tia felt her blood rise. She jabbed at the cake and smashed it with the back of her fork.

Jennifer frowned. "I'm sorry. Did I say something wrong?"

"Yes." Tia took a breath. "You said *was* special. Like she's not coming back."

"Oh … I'm so sorry, Tia. I didn't mean that at all."

"It just bugs me so much, you know?" she said, her voice choking. "Everyone is so sorry and so concerned, but no one is doing anything to find her."

"I'm sure that's not true."

"Yes, it's true!" Tia exploded. "You're concerned, the police are concerned, Cathy is concerned ..." She felt her face getting hot. Why was she so angry? It wasn't Jennifer's fault. She knew that. "Sorry," she mumbled.

"It's okay," Jennifer said. Her voice was gentle. "I think the cake got the worst of it."

Tia glanced down at her plate. Sure enough, it was thoroughly destroyed. She made a face. "Fosters always do."

"Tia!"

"I'm sorry. Another dumb joke."

Jennifer looked at Tia with eyes full of sympathy, but somehow it didn't bug her as much as it usually did. "You know, you shouldn't do that. You shouldn't ... oh, I don't know what I'm trying to say. Let's look at this differently. You see that cake?"

She glanced down at her plate.

"Okay, maybe not that piece. Look at the big cake. See those layers?"

Tia nodded.

"The cookie layers are soft and pretty unremarkable all on their own. But then you add this filling made up of sticky prunes and wonderful spices, and the cake becomes something beautiful and strong. No one knows for sure where the cake came from, but that doesn't even matter. It is special because of all that goes into it."

Tia sat back. "I get what you are saying."

"Good!" she said. Now how about we go for a ride?"

Tia looked up. "You mean on a horse?"

Jennifer grinned. "That's exactly what I mean."

"I don't know how."

"Well since you are working here, don't you think you should learn?"

As Jennifer cleared away the cake, Tia focussed on collecting herself. Riding! Wow.

And then she saw it. Peeking out from beneath a stack of envelopes near Jennifer's laptop. A credit card. Tia's breath caught in her chest. She tried to fight the thought that came to her, to block it, but it pushed through.

A credit card meant money. A credit card could buy travel and a place to stay in Winnipeg. A credit card would fix everything.

"Ready?" Jennifer asked.

Tia blushed and nodded.

Having a bad thought didn't mean anything. People had bad thoughts all the time. It was what you did with them—or didn't do—that mattered.

Tia followed Jennifer to the barn, where they selected saddles and bridles and carried them out to the paddock. In no time, Dinni and Garri were side by side, saddled and ready.

"Go ahead," Jennifer said, holding Dinni by the bridle. "Climb on."

Tia put her left foot in the left stirrup and, just as she'd seen on TV and in movies, swung her right foot over. The saddle was hard and she felt very high up.

"You good?" Jennifer asked.

"Yeah!" she said, a little bit awed.

Jennifer handed Tia the reins, adjusted her stirrups and climbed onto Garri. Side by side, they walked around the edge of the paddock. After a few laps, Jennifer led Tia to the edge and began riding Garri in circles over open ground. Dinni must have been getting bored, as she tossed her head and began to trot. Tia felt herself sliding sideways, despite the smooth gait. "Whoooah," she said, straightening herself and leaning back. Dinni stopped.

"Good job!" Jennifer called. She'd drawn close again while Tia had been otherwise occupied.

Tia beamed.

"Want to try that again? If you're ready."

She nodded. With Jennifer's guidance, she learned how to keep her seat and move from a walk to that strange running-walk called a tolt that Icelandic horses could do.

Afterward, she groomed both horses and then checked in on Disa one last time before heading home.

Home. When had she started to think of the lodge that way?

Chapter Ten

"Come on, Tia, you'll enjoy yourself. We all will!" Cathy said as she spread big goops of egg salad onto slices of whole wheat bread. She wrapped the sandwiches in plastic and placed them in a large, orange cooler bag. "Plus, it's for a very good cause. We get to have fun and the hospital gets much-needed new beds."

Tia took a fluffy, blue bath towel from a large wicker basket and folded it neatly onto the growing stack on the kitchen table. "I'd rather go to the ranch."

Riding Dinni had been wonderful, but that wasn't the only reason she wanted to be there. She loved everything about working there, caring for the animals, making them feel happy and safe. And then there was Disa. She loved that sweet mare so much and wanted to check on her, to see how she was doing.

Cathy raised an eyebrow. "We've talked about this, Tia. You and Tag are part of our family now and we haven't really had a chance to get away for any family-type fun since you arrived."

Tia shrugged, feeling storm clouds gather. "I guess you've been busy with lodge guests."

Cathy picked up on the dig and looked sharply at her.

It was true that the lodge had been busy, but Tia knew her comment was unfair. The time Tia spent at Ice Pony Ranch was at least part of the reason. Cathy could have insisted Tia spend more time helping out at the lodge, but she didn't and Tia didn't offer.

Tag, on the other hand, couldn't wait to pitch in. He'd rush to finish his homework and head down to the boathouse with Bob to take care of fishing rods and lure. Often, when Bob was taking guests out on the lake and there was room left in the boat, Bob would invite him along. At first, Bob had invited Tia too, but she had no interest in stinky fish.

"Come on, Tia," Cathy pressed, as she added juice boxes to the cooler. "It'll be fun. Besides, I could really use your help with the girls."

The real reason Cathy wants me to come along, Tia thought. Now that fake mom trusted her with Summer and Daye, it was like looking after them had suddenly become her job. She pressed her hands into fists, scrunching the towel she was holding.

She could feel Cathy's eyes on her. Tia glanced up. Yep, she was definitely staring.

"Is something wrong?" Cathy asked.

"No," Tia said through clenched teeth. "Everything is fine."

What did it even matter? Her plan to find Richard hadn't panned out—the hotels she'd contacted had been no help at all. And without Richard ...

The words rocketed around and around in her brain like a stone in a dryer. *Without Richard, without Richard, without Richard.*

She unscrunched the towel and folded faster.

"Tia!" Summer cried, bursting into the kitchen and hugging her leg. "Can I help?"

The dark emotion that had begun to build like a summer storm pushed back a little. Then, a little more. None of this had anything to do with Summer or Daye. She picked up another towel. "Sure. You take this side"—she had the little girl hold a corner in each hand—"and I'll fold this side up toward you. And again. See? All done."

Summer giggled and held up her hands for another towel. A moment later, the giggles doubled as Daye joined them. "Me too?" she asked.

"Of course." Tia gave Daye the edges she'd been holding and set the girls folding together.

Cathy leaned close to Tia as she walked past, carrying the cooler to the door. "You are so good with them, Tia," she whispered. "Thank you!"

Tia felt like growling all over again. She liked Summer and Daye. They made her feel like they could be her little sisters for real. Cathy just tried too hard, which only reminded Tia of how separate she and Tag were from this family.

Bob pushed through the swinging door with Tag hot on his heels. "Come on!" he boomed. "Everyone pile in the van."

Reluctant, Tia followed Bob outside and climbed into the third row of seats beside Tag, while Summer and Daye were secured into the second. The ten-minute drive to the community hall felt like an hour. Tia stared out the window the whole time, watching the gravel road disappear behind them and wishing she hadn't been forced to come along.

Cathy twisted in her seat to look at them. "I'm so glad we're all together." She smiled, her eyes glistening.

"Fambly time, fambly time!" Daye chanted while Summer giggled.

Tia rolled her eyes. Great. Cathy had brainwashed the twins with that stupid phrase.

At the hall, everyone tumbled out of the van. Inside and off to one side, there was a makeshift stage with four people, mouths pressed to microphones as they sang and strummed guitars. Beyond the stage, there were food booths set at more or less regular intervals.

"Look!" Daye cried, pointing as they began exploring. "Bouncy Land!"

"I want to do that!" Tag said, pointing toward a booth displaying crude-looking tools with wooden handles. "Can we look at the Viking tools? Please?"

Cathy was already looking harried and Bob was nowhere to be seen. He'd probably seen somebody he knew as they walked and had stopped to chat. He hadn't stopped calling out to people since they arrived.

"No! Bouncy Land!" Daye cried.

"Bouncy Land!" echoed Summer.

"Why don't we do Bouncy Land first and then look at the tools?" Cathy suggested. To Tia, she added, "There's no way Summer and Daye will stand still unless we do it this way."

Sure, Tia thought, resisting the urge to roll her eyes. *Of course.* Cathy said a lot of pretty words about family, but her real children always came first. She watched as Tag swallowed his disappointment.

"Come along, Tia!" Cathy called as Summer and Daye pulled her along. "And don't forget the cooler." She had dropped it in order to clasp hands with each twin.

Tia picked it up, fuming over the fact that Cathy expected her to carry it without even asking. Before she put the strap over her shoulder, she gave the cooler a hard shake, as if to bruise what was inside. She knew it was silly—egg salad sandwiches didn't bruise—but she had to do something. She felt her big, black blob of bad mood grow, grow, grow inside her. Pretty soon it would leak out of her ears.

Tia saw no other choice so she trailed after them. As Cathy and Tag watched Summer and Daye jump madly about the inflated enclosure, Tia daydreamed about what kind of baby Disa would have. Grandpa Bebe had said Disa was still a few weeks away, but it seemed like that's what he said every time Tia asked. Disa must be getting a little closer. Would it be a boy or a girl? Would its colour be like its mom's, or its dad's, or something all its own?

If Cathy hadn't insisted on this stupid family time, she could be at Ice Pony Ranch right now, instead of lugging around coolers and bearing witness to her brother's disappointment.

As she looked around, Tia realized she'd been here before. Three summers ago, in this very hall, for a craft fair with Mama and Tag. Afterward, they'd stopped at the H.P. Tergesen General Store because Mama had wanted a book to read at the nearby beach. There'd been books all right, but also shelves and shelves of toys, candy, dishes, almost anything you could think of. There'd also been a compact mirror with a shiny, blue case that looked like a shell when it snapped shut.

Tia still didn't know what had come over her that day.

After making sure no one was looking—not Mama, not the storekeeper, not her tattletale little brother and not any of the other shoppers—she'd grabbed that mirror and slipped it into her pocket. She'd expected to be stopped by the storekeeper or someone else, but that hadn't happened.

Fearing Mama would never believe she'd just found it if it looked too new, Tia had scooped some gravel from the road, dropped it into her pocket with the mirror and rubbed it around a little. Later, as Mama spread out a blanket and doled out peanut butter sandwiches, Tia pulled the mirror out, smiling big as she revealed her found treasure.

Mama had known, though, like she always did when Tia wasn't being her very best self. She'd marched Tia right back into Tergesen's and made her give it back—along with an apology. Then she'd forced Tia to purchase the mirror using the money she'd earned from walking dogs and weeding gardens around the neighborhood.

Tia kept that mirror as a reminder of the worst thing she'd ever done and would never do again. She kept it until it was taken from her at their first placement. It was cracked and the foster mom said it was dangerous.

Just one more piece of her past, and of her Mama, taken from her.

As Summer and Daye emerged from the Bouncy Land exit, cheeks flushed and grinning, Tia snapped back to the present. Bob reappeared carrying a bag of deep-fried donuts for all.

"Oh, Bob, not until after we have our lunches!" Cathy cried.

Bob looked confused. "Oh. Well then, let's have lunch!" he said, herding them towards the tables and chairs that had been set out.

Tia saw Tag look wistfully at the Viking booth as they walked past it, but he kept his disappointment to himself, just like always. Tia felt her anger flare. It was all she could do to keep herself from dumping the cooler, snatching up Tag's hand and running them both far away from there. She'd promised she wouldn't wreck things for Tag, but why couldn't he see that they were being treated as second best?

She would make him realize that, in time, but not today, not while there was at least a chance he might have fun. Instead, she helped Cathy settle the twins at a picnic table and began passing out the sandwiches and juice.

Tag was silent while munching on his sandwich. He looked like he was pretending to be happy. Tia had seen him like this too many times before.

"Can we go to the Viking booth next?" Tia asked. She saw a spark in her brother's eyes as he looked from her to Cathy and Bob.

"The Viking booth? Why sure, I guess we could," Bob said. "But there are so many things to see! Those old tools aren't going anywhere. We should check the entertainment schedule and see what's on when. We don't want to miss anything."

"The performances for the little kids will be on earlier," Cathy pointed out.

"True, true," Bob said.

Tia couldn't bear to hear another word. Jumping up from the table, she stood, arms straight at her sides, hands balled into fists. "And let me guess," she said, "when those are done, it still won't be a good time. You'll have me and Tag stay home with the twins, while you both come back and dance all night with the rest of the grownups!"

For a moment, Bob and Cathy said nothing. They just stared at Tia, their mouths open in shock. Cathy recovered first. "Tia, honey, what are you talking about? This is a family day!"

"Sure, as long as your name is—" Tia paused, looking at the twins. She didn't want to hurt their feelings, but she was just so mad! "As long as your name doesn't start with *T!*"

Tag frowned.

"I know what starts with *T*," Summer said, giggling.

Tia ignored her. "You know Tag really wanted to go to see the Viking tools, but no, you said he had to wait until after Bouncy Land."

"Yay! Bouncy Land!" Daye cried, clapping her hands. Bob shushed her.

"And now you're making it sound like it's not important at all! Like *we're* not important!" Tia felt her blood rise along with her voice as she tried not to see the growing number of curious looks from the crowd. "Why don't you just admit why we're here? It has nothing to do with family time. Tag and I aren't your family. We're just your babysitters!"

Tag looked at her, his eyes huge and pleading, and Tia clamped her mouth shut. Why had she said that? She loved spending time with the twins! Spinning on her heels, she walked away.

"Tia, wait!" Cathy cried. "That's not true!"

She heard Bob hold her back. "Let her go, Cathy. Let her cool off, first."

Yeah, right, Tia thought. She knew the real reason Bob didn't want to follow. He didn't want to leave the party! Adults were the same everywhere, whether they were your parents by birth or just temporary.

"Tia!" Tag cried, running to catch up. "Where are you going?"

Tia stopped and took him by the hand. "I'm sorry, Tag. I'm really sorry I wrecked things." Her eyes clouded with tears.

"It's okay, Tia. I'm sure you can say sorry, and—"

"Just go back, okay, Tag? Go back and make sure they take you to the Viking booth."

"Where are you going?"

"I don't know." But she did know. "The ranch, maybe." The ache in her was so big, she thought she might break in two.

"But what about family time?" Tag asked.

"Do you really think we're part of this, Tag?" Seeing the hurt in his eyes, she felt awful. And it would get worse, but only for a while. She took a breath. "Look, I'm just in a bad mood, okay? Go back and have fun."

After a moment, he nodded. "Okay. See you later?"

"Of course." As he turned to leave, she grabbed hold of him and hugged him tight. When she finally let go, she couldn't speak.

"You sure you're okay?" he asked.

She ruffled his hair and watched him trot back to the Magnussons. Cathy and Bob watched her, but stayed where they were. Tag must have told them she was going to the ranch because Cathy nodded and then waved to her, as if everything was fine.

Instead of walking along the highway, Tia took the path along the edge of the lake and then another path that joined the highway much farther along. Finally, she was at the lodge.

In the kitchen, she paused to look at the table, where conversations had been shared, homework finished and laundry folded. Normal family-type stuff. The ache in Tia's throat increased, making it hard to swallow.

At the computer, she made one last check of her email. Nothing from the hotels. The ember of remaining hope she'd held so tight fizzled and snuffed out.

Truth settled in its place.

Richard was not really a hotel owner and maybe he didn't even work at one. She guessed she always knew that. He was just a guy. Someone Mama knew for a while and then let go. Temporary, just like everyone and everything else.

None of that mattered. What happened next was up to her.

Walking up the hall to her room, she said a silent thank you to the Magnussons for all they'd given her and Tag. Now that she'd made her decision, it was somehow easier to remember all of the other nice things—like the backpacks and the help with homework, and how Bob had spent time with Tag fixing up that old bike and then let him keep it. Even Cathy, really, hadn't been that bad. When she and Tia talked, Cathy had really listened to her. Tia could tell that she was hearing and thinking about everything Tia said. Even the mean things.

In her room, she pulled out her backpack and sat on her bed.

Finally, she let her tears fall. They would be the last she allowed herself, she decided. She knew Tag would be devastated, but she had to do something and this was the only thing left. She would go to Winnipeg and find Mama.

When she put their family, their *real* family, back together, Tag would forgive her.

Tia was the only one who cared enough to get this done, the only one who would turn every stone, follow every lead, until Mama was found. It wouldn't be easy, especially without Richard, but she had no choice.

Better she did this now than wait until Cathy finally had enough of her and sent both her and Tag somewhere else. For all Cathy's faults, Tia knew she would never split up a brother and sister. But Tag liked it here. And this family liked Tag.

The pain in her heart threatened to split her in two.

From her school notebook, she tore a blank page and wrote a note for Tag.

I love you. I am going to find Mama.

Quickly, not wanting to lose her resolve, she placed the note on Tag's bed, packed a change of clothes and her treasure box in her backpack and left.

At the Ice Pony Ranch and Animal Rescue Centre, Tia ducked behind a leafy tree just outside the paddock fence. Grandpa Bebe was riding Garri. She couldn't let him see her—he might have questions she wasn't prepared to answer—but she needed to visit Disa one last time.

She looked to the house to make sure Jennifer wasn't looking out the window. Scanning the yard, she realized her truck wasn't even there. Good.

Tia dashed to the barn, looking again at the kitchen window. An idea sparked, big and terrible.

What was that old saying? Desperate times call for desperate measures. Like Mama said, sometimes that meant doing things you never thought you would.

She ran across the yard to the house, shooting a quick glance over her shoulder to make sure no one would take that moment to come up the drive or walk around the corner, then she let herself in.

Just like every other time she'd been there, Jennifer's laptop was open on the table, a stack of notes and envelopes next to it.

Hands shaking, she moved the envelopes around.

It wasn't there.

There were drawers in the counter close by where Jennifer worked. She opened one. Electrical looking stuff. No good. She opened another. Scissors, a stapler, paperclips and a small cardboard box.

She opened the box.

Inside, there was a chequebook, stamps and a credit card.

She peeked out the window—still no one—and snatched the credit card, stuck it in her back pocket and dashed to the door.

The credit card felt hot in her pocket. But she needed it. Finding Mama was more important than anything else and a credit card would take her a lot further than the few dollars she'd earned working at the shelter.

Her hand was on the doorknob. Why couldn't she turn it?

"Because this isn't who I am," she said out loud.

It's not who Mama brought her up to be.

She returned the credit card to the box and left the house.

Grandpa Bebe and Garri were still in the back paddock. Making sure she remained unseen, Tia opened the barn door and slipped inside.

She breathed in the warm scent of sweet hay and horse sweat, heavy with the realization this would be her last time here.

She stopped briefly to see Dinni first. "You're such a good girl," she whispered, "keeping your mama company when I know you'd rather be outside playing in the paddock."

Disa gave a whinny and banged against the stall. Tia looked up. "Just a minute, Disa!" she called. "I'm saving my longest visit for you."

Poor girl. It was hard for her to be cooped up so long. As she left Dinni for Disa's stall, Tia heard a groan and a loud thump.

Disa was lying on her side with her legs pushed out straight. The straw was wet, as if she'd peed quite a lot, but it smelled funny.

"What's wrong girl?" Realization dawned on her. "The baby!"

Tia felt a white-hot lightning bolt shoot through her, though she wasn't sure if it was excitement or panic. "Hang on, girl, I'll go get Grandpa Bebe!"

She pounded down the aisle toward the door that led out to the first paddock. "Grandpa Bebe!" she shouted, flinging the door wide open.

It was a mistake.

As if in slow motion, Tia saw the paddock, then Garri's head, shoulders and legs as he reared up, Grandpa Bebe beside him ... and Grandpa Bebe's hand, caught up in Garri's lead rope, as he was pulled off his feet.

"Garri! No!" Tia screamed. It only made things worse. Garri bolted, dragging Grandpa Bebe behind him.

Chapter Eleven

In a moment, it was over. Grandpa Bebe had managed to get his hand loose, but he was lying on the ground at an unusual angle, not moving. Garri was standing a few feet away, head held high, nostrils flared.

"Grandpa Bebe!" Tia felt her voice catch in her throat as she ran over, sat down beside him and gently touched his left arm, the one that wasn't twisted so horribly. Garri moved close and snuffled Grandpa Bebe's face while Scout licked his ear.

"Please," Tia begged, hiccoughing and sniffling. "You have to be okay." Relief washed over her as Grandpa Bebe's eyes fluttered open.

"Hi Tia," he said weakly. He tried to sit up, but winced in pain. "Just wrenched my arm a bit."

"I'm so sorry, Grandpa Bebe! It's my fault!" Tia cried, tears running freely down her cheeks. "I didn't call through the door. I scared Garri." She sat on her knees beside him, holding her head in her hands. Why, oh why couldn't she do anything right? Everything she touched turned into a steaming pile of screw-up, even when she was trying to help.

"I wasn't expecting you today."

"It's Disa, Grandpa Bebe! I think she's having her foal!"

Grunting, Grandpa Bebe sat up straighter. "Really?" he asked. "Well, how about that." He patted his jacket pocket with his left hand and then scanned the paddock. "Get my phone, Tia," he said, pointing to where he'd dropped it. "And help me up."

Tia obeyed, feeling like her own knees would buckle when he cried out in pain. "Isn't it too soon, Grandpa Bebe? You said she wasn't due for a few more weeks."

Grandpa Bebe stood awkwardly, his right arm hanging limp beside him. "It is early, Tia, but possible."

Tia swallowed. She wanted to shout for help and run wildly down the highway. But this was no time to lose it. Instead, she pushed all her panic and worry into a damp ball at the bottom of her stomach until only urgency remained. "Her stall is all wet and it smells funny."

"What do you mean, 'funny'?"

She thought. "Kind of sweet."

Grandpa Bebe nodded. "Let's have a look. Sounds like her water broke."

"Is that good?"

"It's as it should be."

Tia felt relief flood through her. For Disa, at least. Grandpa Bebe was walking slowly, as if every breath caused him pain.

At the stall, Grandpa Bebe peered inside. He punched numbers on the phone with his thumb and held it to his ear. "Jennifer? I need you to come home, honey. Looks like Disa is having her foal —" He paused to listen. "A bit early, yeah. Disa does like to follow her own schedule, hey?" He chuckled. "All right, see you soon."

"How come you didn't tell her about your arm." Tia asked after Grandpa Bebe had hung up the phone.

"I'll tell her when she gets here. No sense having her fussing over the phone."

"Okay. Now what?"

"Now we just stay quiet and watch."

"Shouldn't we call the vet?" she asked.

"Nah, not necessary. Horses foal all the time, often when no one is around to watch. This is pretty special."

Tia let a sense of goodness enter her. Disa was going to be okay. Grandpa Bebe was going to be okay. And in this moment, this was exactly where she was meant to be.

Too bad Tag wasn't here to share this. Actually, Cathy might like it more.

Tia gave her head a shake. *Why would I want to share anything with Cathy, especially something as special as this?*

She couldn't think about that now. Too confusing. Instead, she concentrated on what was happening in the birthing stall. Disa stood, turned, and lay down again. On her side, the horse strained and strained, slick with sweat. Tia jumped as the mare suddenly rolled to her other side and then back again.

Then it happened. Tia spotted a white bubble coming out of the horse, followed by a tiny hoof. Behind the hoof, there was the start of a black leg. She felt shivers up and down her entire body. She felt like crying, though she didn't know why. "The baby!"

Grandpa Bebe grinned, eyes sparkling, looking every bit as happy and excited as Tia. They watched as Disa rested for a moment, then strained with the next contraction. The leg and the hoof stayed where they were.

Disa strained again, but the foal progressed no further.

Tia glanced up at Grandpa Bebe. His forehead was creased with a deep frown line.

"Is something wrong?" she whispered.

His answer took a long time, like it was stuck behind his tongue. Finally, he said, "Yes, Tia, I think there might be."

Alarm shot through her. "What?"

Grandpa Bebe took his phone back out and punched at the numbers with his thumb. "I'm not sure." He put the phone to his ear. "Yes, this is a message for Dr. Jacobs. My mare is in labour, but she's having trouble. I think the foal might be in the wrong position." He listened. "I'd check myself, but I've banged up my arm. Please tell him to come as fast as he can." He touched his thumb to the phone, ending the call.

"Is it bad?" Tia asked, her stomach twisting in a knot.

"He's out on another emergency." Grandpa Bebe held his pointer finger up, motioning for her to wait just a minute, and then used his thumb to punch another number into the cellphone. "Jennifer? Where are you?" He listened for a moment, then sighed heavily and shook his head. "Okay, just get here as fast as you can, okay?"

He put his phone in his pocket and looked at Tia with eyes narrowed, as if deciding something.

"Why didn't you tell Jennifer what's happening?"

"Semi jackknifed on the highway. Traffic's backed up. There's nothing she can do to get here any faster."

"But the foal is in the wrong position!" Tia exclaimed. "What can we do?"

"It's what *you're* going to do, Tia."

Tia felt the world fall away. "Me?"

"The foal is probably stopped because its knee is bent. It needs be straight for it to come out. I need you to go in and check."

"What do you mean, go in?"

With his good arm, Grandpa Bebe opened a box next to Disa's stall and pulled out disinfectant hand jelly, latex gloves and lubricant. "Clean your hands and arms really good with this first," he said, handing her the jelly. "Then put on the gloves. You've got to reach in beside the foal and check its position."

"What?" Tia choked out.

Disa lifted her head, then thumped it back down, groaning loudly.

"But it'll be ... gross." It was a stupid thing to say, even though it was true. Never in her life had she ever thought she would put her hands inside a living creature. The idea of it made her want to upchuck. And beyond that, what if she screwed up? This beautiful mare ... She watched Disa panting, her kind, dark eyes showing white along the edges as she grunted and moaned.

"Tia, you can do it. You're good with horses. It won't be as hard as you think."

"No. No, I can't, Grandpa Bebe!" The idea of doing something that might hurt Disa was more than she could bear.

"Yes, you can. I'll be right here."

Tia shook her head frantically. "You don't understand! Everything I touch and everything I do and even everything I *say* turns out wrong." She felt tears gather.

"Please, Tia." Grandpa Bebe pleaded. "I need you to focus. Think about Disa. We don't know when the vet will get my message, and if Jennifer doesn't get here soon enough ..." His voice trailed off.

"What?"

"We could lose the foal. Maybe Disa too."

Tia stopped breathing. "She could die?"

Grandpa Bebe was more serious than she'd even seen him. "Yes, Tia, that's what I mean."

Swallowing hard, Tia looked at the gloves, then at Disa, then at the tiny, little hoof. Disa thrust her legs straight out once again, groaning, but still there was no further sign of the foal.

"The longer we wait, the more Disa is going to contract and the tighter it's going to get for the baby."

Tia thought of that tiny hoof and the little horse it was attached to and wondered if it was frightened. What must it be like? What if being born was like moving toward daylight, but then suddenly everything stopped? What if the poor thing could see what it wanted, where it was supposed to go, but couldn't get to it? Forget frightened, it must be terrified.

"Tia?"

She looked solemnly at Grandpa Bebe. There was a tension in him she'd never seen before. Fear showed in his face, his breathing, even in the way he held his hands and shoulders. He loved these horses so much. He loved Disa. So did Tia.

Of course she would help. She would try with everything in her. Whatever it took.

She nodded.

Oh, please do not screw this up! If she was ever going to get anything right, it had to be this. Two lives depended on it.

Tia did as Grandpa Bebe instructed, washing from her fingertips all the way up her arms. She pulled on the gloves and moved quietly toward Disa. "It's okay, Big Mama," she crooned. "I'm just here to help you with the baby."

Taking a deep breath, Tia reached in and felt along the length of the foal's leg. After a moment, she no longer felt awkward or weird. This was a real, live foal! And she was going to help it be born.

"Just the one leg," she told Grandpa Bebe. "And its head!"

Tia felt like she might cry. This baby—living, slick, hot to her touch, ready to breathe its first breath—needed her help. What was it thinking? Did it know that its life was literally in her hands?

Then she felt it. A tiny pulse. Fast.

"Tia?"

Grandpa Bebe's voice sounded far away. Though it shouldn't be possible, now she could hear the pulse, loud, inside her head, the baby's heart beating hard and quick, as if to match her own.

The baby. Heart beating with hers. It was like they were one.

Time stopped.

She couldn't move.

"Tia? Tia, honey. What's wrong? Can you hear me?" His voice echoed, sounding far away.

Tia felt cold. Dizzy.

She heard Grandpa Bebe again, stronger this time. "Stay with me, Tia. Focus."

"Yes," Tia said, her voice weak. She cleared her throat. "I'm okay." Suddenly a feeling of warmth and rightness infused her. She felt stronger. She felt *back*.

"You sure? You looked pretty pale for a minute there."

"Yes," she said again. Everything was going to be fine. She would make sure of it.

"Okay, sounds like baby has a bent knee. You need to push the foal back in and then reach inside Mama and straighten the baby's leg. Can you do that, Tia?"

Tia nodded, terrified but determined. "I can, Grandpa Bebe. I'll try." No, that wasn't good enough. She set her jaw. "I mean, I will."

"I'm not worried a bit." His voice sounded calm and reassuring, as if he had just told her the right way to pick out hooves.

Tia took a deep breath and then gently pushed until the baby was all the way back inside. She heard Disa groan. "Just a minute, Mama! Don't contract yet."

As quickly as she could but with utmost care, she reached in with her hand, felt along the foal's leg to where it was bent and then pulled it forward. "Got it!"

"Make sure one leg is lined up a little behind the other," Grandpa Bebe advised. "Its shoulders should be angled coming out."

Disa groaned again and Tia felt the mare's body go rigid. She got out of the way as Disa contracted and the tiny hoof appeared once more. This time, a second hoof followed it.

"Good girl, Tia!" Grandpa Bebe cheered. "You did it!"

Tia began to cry as the whole foal appeared. She blinked each fat, blubbery tear away, hardly noticed them except when they blurred the miracle in front of her. She felt a warm glow wash through her.

She had just witnessed a miracle. Her. The girl nobody wanted.

Not even Mama.

Through her tears, Tia watched Disa lovingly nudge her baby. A mother looked after her babies. Like Cathy did for the twins. Like she did for Tia and Tag too, even though she wasn't their real mother.

Tia had been so mad at her.

Watching Disa and the baby, Grandpa Bebe close beside her, Tia felt a tiny glimmer of understanding. Maybe it had been there all along.

It wasn't Cathy she was mad at. It was Mama.

Mama had always said she would come back, but this time she hadn't. Maybe she never would. In her heart, Tia knew she wasn't waiting to be found. That was just what Tia had told herself so that she could hang on to hope.

But Mama wasn't coming back. Whatever the reason, she just wasn't.

Tia didn't hate her for it. She couldn't. She'd seen the goodness in Mama no one else had. The playful and singing bits, the telling her she could do anything bits.

But there'd also been the not-so-good bits.

She wasn't the same mama she'd been before Daddy had died: the mama Tag had never seen, the one Tia still remembered. It wasn't fair that Tag never got the good mama, but she'd left them both a long time ago.

It hurt to think that, because, in spite of everything, Tia still loved her and missed her and was so worried about her.

Mama was gone, but goodness still happened. Like baby horses and helping one take its first breath.

Tia turned and hugged Grandpa Bebe tight but gently, so as not to disturb his hurt arm. Disa stood and the white sack that had been covering the foal was pulled away.

He was tiny, jet black, and absolutely perfect.

Chapter Twelve

When Tia called, Cathy squealed with excitement. She also said she'd been worried about Tia and was so glad to hear her voice.

"They're coming over," Tia told to Grandpa Bebe, handing him back his phone. "All of them. I hope that's okay."

"As long as we keep things quiet," he said.

Grandpa Bebe's attempted smile turned into a grimace and Tia remembered his arm. "Does it hurt a lot? What can I do?"

Before he could answer, there was a muffled call of "Door!" and Jennifer hurried into the barn. The broad smile she'd entered with fell away as she looked at her father, his pain obvious. Scout, who'd been shut outside in the excitement, was hot on her heels, wagging his tail extra hard as if to say he forgave them for leaving him out.

Jennifer glanced in Disa's stall as she passed but went straight to Grandpa Bebe, her face full of concern.

In a rush, Tia's shame of taking Jennifer's credit card came back. The urge to flee was so strong, Tia felt the muscles in her calves tighten.

She held her ground, forcing her body to stay put. She was through with running away, but she could step outside. "I'll watch for Cathy and Bob," Tia said, patting her leg for Scout to follow.

Despite Cathy saying she'd been worried, Tia wasn't at all sure she'd be happy to see her—not after the things Tia had said. She would face her outside, away from the beautiful gift she'd just been part of. Cathy would either tell her she'd had enough and was sending her away or she would take her back home to the lodge.

Home to the lodge. The old key she'd hung onto from their apartment didn't seem to matter much anymore. After all, some other family had moved in and all of Tia, Tag and Mama's belongings had been disposed of or sold by the landlord to pay for what they owed him in rent.

Home was more than where you hung your hat. It was where people cared for you, and where you wanted to be because you cared for them too.

"Would you mind watching for the vet, Tia?" Jennifer asked. "I need to take Dad in for x-rays."

"That'll wait," Grandpa Bebe said.

"Dad, I swear you are more stubborn than a mule."

Tia made a wish that this not be the last time she heard Jennifer and Grandpa Bebe's gentle teasing, and then she went outside.

She sat on bench as nerves fluttered in her stomach. Petting Scout, she found comfort in his warmth as he leaned against her legs.

When the van pulled into the yard, Scout jogged over to greet the family, tail wagging.

The twins giggled and chattered, pulling Bob past Tia and into the barn, while Cathy and Tag hung back, greeting the horses on the other side of the fence. Tag cast furtive glances toward her as he tore handfuls of tall grass and fed the horses. Tia watched as Cathy put her hand on Tag's shoulder and said something she couldn't hear.

Cathy stayed by the fence as Tag walked toward Tia, head down.

"What's up, little bro?" she asked, casting a worried glance toward Cathy. Had she told Tag to deliver the terrible news?

But when Tag lifted his eyes to hers, she was startled to see them full of hurt and betrayal.

"You left me," he said.

The note. With all that had happened, she'd forgotten about her note. "No, Tag, I didn't leave you," she said gently and reached for his hand. He pulled it away. She felt a stab of pain. "I mean, not forever."

"You left me. Just like Mama did."

"No! Tag, no. It's not the same thing."

"Yes, it is. You don't care. You only care about yourself."

"But I ..." her protest died on her lips. "You're right." The truth of it settled into her bones. She'd been so focussed on Mama that she hadn't thought enough about Tag. He needed to know that the people he loved didn't always leave. She sighed. "I was a jerk."

Tag seemed to consider this, then he sat beside her. "Do you think Mama's ever coming back?"

She drew in a deep breath before answering. "I don't know." Tears stung her eyes. "But probably not."

They hugged each other. "I made her mad, Tag. The night before she left."

"She was always mad, Tia. She didn't go because of that."

The simplicity and truth of her brother's words brought bigger tears, ones that were impossible to hold back. She hugged him tighter.

"You can't leave me anymore, Tia."

"I won't," she said, clearing her throat. "I promise."

"Okay." He pulled away, smiling like sunshine. "Can I go see the baby horse now?"

She ruffled his hair. "Of course."

As Tag went into the barn, Tia wiped away her tears. Cathy joined her, taking Tag's place on the bench. Tia took a deep breath, willing her nerves to settle.

"I heard what you said to Tag. About the possibility that your mother may not come back." Her voice was gentle. Not what Tia had expected. "That must have been hard to say to him. Is that what you believe?"

"I don't know."

"Tag showed us your note."

She swallowed. "I thought I could find her, you know? It didn't seem like anyone was looking hard enough."

"You must have felt so alone. Why didn't you come to us?"

"I think maybe … I was angry and afraid that if I let myself be a family with you, if I let you help me like a mom, it was like I was saying … I don't know. That my mom wasn't as good. And that felt awful. I've been awful. To you. I'm sorry."

"Oh, Tia. Not so awful as you think." Cathy drew her into a hug. It felt good and right. She hugged back.

"Will you help me?" Tia asked. "I need to know they won't stop looking for her."

"They won't," Cathy said. "We won't. Yes, we'll help."

Something warm sparked in her belly and spread up and through every part of her. "Thank you."

Cathy gave her one more squeeze, then pulled away, bright-eyed. "Should we go inside? I'd like to see this foal."

Together, they re-entered the barn and joined Bob, Grandpa Bebe and Jennifer next to Disa's stall. The office door was open and Tia could see Tag, Summer and Daye playing some sort of game that involved circling around the desk. Scout sat in the doorway, panting, his tongue lolling out the side of his mouth. He looked happy.

Scout had known right from the beginning that this was his home. Animals were smart that way.

"He's beautiful," Cathy breathed, looking at the foal. "What's his name?"

Grandpa Bebe looked to Jennifer, who smiled and nodded. "What would you call him, Tia?" Grandpa Bebe asked.

"Me? Isn't there some sort of Icelandic naming rule?"

"You've earned the honour," Jennifer said. "Besides, there are the names we put on the registration, and then there are the names we actually use."

"A rose by any other name, and all that," Bob offered.

A rose made her think of flowers, like the sunflowers Mama had grown in her garden, and later the tiny blossoms she'd plucked from between sidewalk cracks. "Maybe not a rose, but—" She looked at him again, the proud arch to his neck. "Do you know the Icelandic word for 'Prince'?"

Jennifer grinned. "I believe that is Baldur. A fine name!"

The swirling, giggling force that was Summer and Daye spun out of the office and sprinted down the aisle toward the door, followed closely by Tag and Scout. As soon as they were out, the door swung open again. It was Tag. "Grandpa Bebe! It's the silly buttheads! They opened the gate again."

"Oh, those horses!"

A few minutes later, they were all laughing, herding the horses back up the drive and into the paddock.

As they returned to the barn, Tia hung back as the others went inside. Her hand on the door handle, she turned, taking in the ranch, the woods and the sky, and she remembered when she'd first come upon it, how it'd felt like walking into a painting, where anything might happen. And something had.

Maybe this wasn't the family she and Tag were born into, but it felt good and warm and safe.

Scout bounded up, his mouth open and, with tongue lolling, he jumped up so that his paws were against her shoulders. Panting, he looked her in the eyes. Tia grinned, bracing herself so that she wasn't pushed over. "What's up, pup?"

Scout licked one cheek, then the other, before settling back on his haunches by her feet. She giggled. "Good answer!"

Horatio hurried from around the side, bleating. Tia held the door and he and Scout scooted inside.

A croak pulled her gaze skyward as the silhouette of a raven crossed the sinking sun. She breathed deep as a breeze kissed her cheek, rustling through leaves. A warmth washed through her.

In the fading light, the shadow that had clung to her for so long lengthened and let go.

Endir

Ostaslaufur
(Traditional Icelandic Cheese Bow Tie Buns)

Adapted from recipe courtesy of Anna Birgis Hannesson, Reykjavik, Iceland, wife of retired Ambassador Hjalmar Hannesson

1 1/3 cups warm milk

4 tsp. instant dry yeast

4 cups all-purpose flour

2 tbs. sugar

1 ½ tsp. salt

½ cups butter, melted

Filling:

1 cup cream cheese, softened

½ cup mozzarella cheese, grated

- In a medium bowl, add yeast to warm milk and let it dissolve.

- Add flour, sugar, salt and butter and knead until elastic. If using an electric mixer, knead on low for 4 minutes, then medium for another 4.

- Let the dough rest in a bowl covered with a damp cloth for 45 min. or until it has doubled in size.

- Roll the dough into a (approx) 24 × 10-inch rectangle.

- Mix softened cream cheese with the grated mozzarella cheese.

- Spread the cheese evenly in the middle of the long length, so that the rectangle is separated by long thirds. Fold one third of one long edge inward to cover the cheese third. Then fold the remaining third over all the way to the first edge. Put a little water along the dough edge and press to seal. Turn the dough so that the seam is down.

- Cut the 24-inch length into 1 ½ to 2 inch strips (makes 8 to 10 strips). Twist each strip to form a "butterfly".

- Place strips on a parchment paper and let rise for 45 min.

- Bake in a preheated oven at 425 °F for about 17-20 minutes.

- Enjoy!

Takk!

No book is an island, and this one would have been adrift without the kindness of many good and talented people. I must first express deepest gratitude to my agent, Marie Campbell, who shores me when I flag and believes in me, always.

Like the early Icelandic settlers of Manitoba's New Iceland, *Forgetting How to Breathe* had a long journey. Its seeds took root over a decade ago with one pivotal scene written while I was writer-in-residence at the now-defunct Aqua Books in Winnipeg, MB. Thank you to Kelly Hughes, owner of Aqua Books; Dr. Tom Pisz, owner of North Country Stables in Yellowknife, who introduced our family to Icelandic horses; Brett Arnason, of Arnason's Icelandic Horse Farm, who graciously answered questions, allowed me to visit, and who—by the way—was instrumental in bringing the first Icelandic horses to Manitoba in 1989; Robbie Rousseau, who reached across the ocean to family friend Anna Birgis Hannesson, who shared her recipe for Ostaslaufur; the Chan family and their exceptional photographer, David Jordan from Leeds, UK, for the breathtaking cover image. So beautiful.

Thank you to my trusted readers: Merry Franz, Kathryn Gamble, Breanna Smith, Fred Penner and Cam Patterson. An extra thank you to Cam, who mentored me through the process of adapting this novel into a screenplay. In writing the story in a new way, I discovered unexpected elements, which fed back into the novel.

My love and gratitude to several significant people whose names I borrowed for characters, something I often do as tribute: my mother and father, Cathy and Bob; my great-great-grandparents John and Gudny Magnus (Magnusson), who immigrated to Canada from Iceland in the late 1800s; Johan Jacobs, who is not a vet, but knows his way around a horse; Bebe Ivanochko, a fiery and inspirational champion of literacy, now gone but never forgotten; and real-life Scout-the-dog, who for many years was official greeter and unofficial mascot at Great Plains Publications. His joyous nature infused fictional Scout from the get-go.

Thank you to the entire team at Great Plains Publications for believing in this story, and most especially my editor, Catharina de Bakker, for her patience, keen eye and deep insights.

Final thanks, as always, to my family, my greatest support: Jim, Erin, and Sara, for laughter and love; my mother and father, Bob and Cathy; my sisters, Heather and Merry; in-laws, niece, nephews, cousins, uncles and aunts, with a special nod to my Aunt Sharon, who inspires me through her own love of books and storytelling.